KISSING A TREE SURGEON

SHORT STORIES

GUERNICA WORLD EDITIONS 31

KISSING A
TREE SURGEON

SHORT STORIES

ELEANOR LEVINE

GUERNICA
World
EDITIONS

TORONTO—CHICAGO—BUFFALO—LANCASTER (U.K.)
2020

Michael Mirolla, general editor
Margo LaPierre, editor
Cover design: Allen Jomoc Jr.
Interior layout: Jill Ronsley, suneditwrite.com
Cover image: *Languor* by Brian Healey
Guernica Editions Inc.
287 Templemead Drive, Hamilton (ON), Canada L8W 2W4
2250 Military Road, Tonawanda, N.Y. 14150-6000 U.S.A.
www.guernicaeditions.com

Distributors:
Independent Publishers Group (IPG)
600 North Pulaski Road, Chicago IL 60624
University of Toronto Press Distribution,
5201 Dufferin Street, Toronto (ON), Canada M3H 5T8
Gazelle Book Services, White Cross Mills
High Town, Lancaster LA1 4XS U.K.

First edition.
Printed in Canada.

Legal Deposit—Third Quarter
Library of Congress Catalog Card Number: 2020934507
Library and Archives Canada Cataloguing in Publication
Title: Kissing a tree surgeon : short stories / Eleanor Levine.
Names: Levine, Eleanor, author.
Series: Guernica world editions ; 31.
Description: Series statement: Guernica world editions ; 31
Identifiers: Canadiana (print) 20200203061 | Canadiana (ebook)
20200203134 | ISBN 9781771835602   (softcover) | ISBN 9781771835619
(EPUB) | ISBN 9781771835626 (Kindle)
Classification: LCC PS3612.E923855 K67 2020 | DDC 813/.6—dc23

For Hilda and Jack

Love is an abstract noun, something nebulous.
And yet love turns out to be the only part of us
that is solid, as the world turns upside down and
the screen goes black.

—Martin Amis,
The Second Plane: 14 Responses to September 11

Without Sexual Attraction

Without sexual attraction, there is
the brutal movement of the sea.
The face peers out of its skeletal frame
and hands reach like bone.
Without love, the streets
are hollow sounding
with wooden, hurried steps,
voices like caverns of death.
We pass each other as trains do,
whistling screams.

—David Ignatow

CONTENTS

LITERARY MENTORS

My FATHER HAD AN UNORTHODOX way of eating apples. He'd crunch with excessive force, so you could hear every piece of apple dispensed in his mouth. His chomping disrupted any sense of decorum at our table, for he believed more in anarchism and nonconformity than in providing us with good dinner etiquette.

This was so unlike my mother who had an adroit seriousness with all things. Seriousness, religiosity—these were my mother.

This protracted seriousness made me so crazy that I ran around the house, the neighborhood, the inner city—crying, screaming, unkempt, taking on a planetary wildness of my own. I yelled at her and my brothers and attacked innocent life forms with a high-pitched voice that could have been the aborted fetus of Beverly Sills.

* * *

I endeavored to be in honors English, read good novels, but when my friend Hank begrudgingly gave me his honors English syllabus, I struggled to complete the assigned book, *Our Mutual Friend,* in one evening.

I never finished *Our Mutual Friend,* and when the English teacher, Mr. FF, asked me to reveal the pathology of the literary man with a wooden leg, I could not.

I didn't want to peruse hundreds of pages, but the alternative was a mediocre classroom challenged by plebeians who were not uplifted by Hemingway or the Brontë sisters. They'd rather read the gory details of Upton Sinclair's *The Jungle* and call it literature.

* * *

I vicariously entered honors English and its symbolisms, bending my ear in the hallway when Mrs. Q, junior year, elucidated the meaning of *Catcher in the Rye*. "Holden Caulfield is a Jesus character wearing a mitt to catch all the innocent kids."

With my ilk, we barely made it through when Holden says the F word. My instructor, Mr. Stray, was fixated on writing a Broadway script, not surmising whether Holden Caulfield was an adolescent savior.

It was particularly tortuous when my supposed "friend" Hank (honors English sycophant and favorite of my mother's) bragged recently about *what great instructors* Mrs. Q and Mr. FF were.

"We were lucky to have them," he said, repeating this sentiment, though we are now in our fifties.

I did not have any literary mentors, particularly in freshman year, because my dullard/teacher said my B average and inability to deliver *Call of the Wild* soliloquies would exclude me from honors English the following year.

I was with intermediate kids who picked on me but acknowledged I made brilliant remarks about *Call of the Wild*, though never brilliant enough for our Jack London instructor who said that, if mediocrity was good enough for her, it was good enough for me.

* * *

Our high school made us return as adults in 2007 because technically we had never graduated. We needed refresher courses in English, science and mathematics. I, for example, had never taken a chemistry course or written about Chaucer.

* * *

Mother's attentions, it seems, were magnified toward Hank when all of us obligingly reported for homeroom in the new millennium; she drove him but asked me to take the bus.

* * *

During high school, the original one in the eighties, I declined to ignore my insanity and promised the world it would hear me lamenting/moaning, and Dad, chewing his apple, queried: "What will the neighbors think?"

"Fuck the neighbors," I said, realizing that Hank and my mother would not include me as a guest at dinner that evening.

* * *

A tornado of post-pubescent fires burned inside me.

In the seventies, I felt suicidal—that the walls might burn—I was with people who threw spitballs and repeated badly thought-out opinions of mine during Holocaust class.

My history teacher, who resembled Attila the Hun, and whom we called "Professor Attila the Hun," berated me. "You never know what you are talking about."

On the first day of class she pulled my ponytail and said: "Someone with your low IQ need not act smart!"

She, with gray moustache and bald spot, was educated at the New Jersey College for Women, and could cite most events from the French Revolution.

"What the hell are you talking about?" she said. "Roosevelt couldn't bomb the trains going to Auschwitz—he'd have killed the Jews. *Are you nuts?*"

Laughter filled the Holocaust class where two teenagers—a future admiral and adulterous lawyer—sat.

"Bomb the trains!" these young men said whenever I spoke. They were convinced I meant: "Bomb the trains, kill the Jews, kill the Nazis, but at least you kill the fucking Nazis."

These boys, budding Kierkegaards, couldn't tolerate my pseudo-intellectualism, certainly not when they were sixteen and knew all the answers.

* * *

The above brutes did not return to high school in 2007. The "admiral" was killed during the Gulf War because he didn't tie his shoes and slipped on an oil spill, banging his head into a nuclear missile. The "lawyer/adulterous chap," who fornicated with his female client's husband, had his Connecticut law license revoked and could not get it unrevoked, though his mother was the president of the Connecticut Bar in New Britain. Indeed, the *faygelah* attorney was so imbued with a sense of smug morality, he decided, prior to the Ebola virus outbreak, to set up a law office in Liberia and have sex with as many naked men per night as possible. It is unclear if he is still in Liberia, or perhaps the remains of his body are floating in the ocean.

* * *

Those who eagerly returned to school in 2007, as if they had never left, were the passive-aggressive ones who said they didn't do well on their tests, but would ultimately receive the ninety-six, in comparison to my unstudied seventy-two. Hank was in the passive-aggressive realm, and my mother never failed to remind me that she should have traded my egg for his.

Whereas Hank believed his uncle—an ex-devotee of the Church of Scientology (who also disputed if there was an equator)—was "completely unsuited to open-mindedness, and did a poor job raising me."

"He'd rather I read *People Magazine* than watch the news," Hank said, whereas my mother made us watch Walter Cronkite every night, faithfully, even when presidents got shot.

Hank wanted the solemnity of my mother and she wanted him.

Hank's legal guardian, Uncle Henry, was my friend, and I discussed these matters, that is, *why my mother—and not me—*was invited to Hank's graduation party in 2007. You'd think Hank would have adjusted his attitude, but he was still as belligerent as he was in the first high school era.

Uncle Henry listened patiently to my dissing Mother and his nephew. "They never include me—think they're better than—*even though I have an MFA in Creative Writing!*"

* * *

In 2007, as I entered Mrs. Q's honors English class, she asked: "Why are you here?" I was stupefied and couldn't muster the correct adjectives. I left.

* * *

Nothing in this middle-aged world, or in my former teen existence, explained why Mother would align herself with Hank. Yes, *mi madre*, that poor insufferable creature who was once clunked on the head by a milk bottle by an irate ex-lover, fussed over the vacuous Hank.

* * *

Uncle Henry, for as long as his nephew knew him, instructed Hank: "Take Agatha along," as if I were the candy-striped charity case serial killer.

Hank, however, wouldn't call me on his rotary phone, particularly if my mother was driving him and there was a sale at Macy's. I was asked to come along only if the destination was ShopRite, and they needed help carrying groceries.

Henry, following our three-month high school internment in 2007, invited me to vacation with him, Hank and Hank's lover Finn in Connecticut. "It's my graduation present to Hank!"

"Yeah, but technically we graduated in *1983*," I said.

"Hank says I've been neglectful—I'm hoping this trip offsets my bad parenting."

In 2007, hence, when the weather was mild in comparison to the snowy New Jersey frost, we entered the Mark Twain House in Hartford, Connecticut, where the author kept leather bound notebooks.

In Twain's bedroom, which consisted of two beds and a wooden desk, I felt as abandoned as I had thirty years ago in Zionist summer camp in the Catskill Mountains when the girls made me sleep in my own tent, and the wind blew ferociously, though it was summer.

"It would have been no different with Palestinian girls," my mother said at the time. "They wouldn't have slept with you either. You have zero social skills."

At Mark Twain's house, Finn was with Hank; Henry was devoted to their happiness; and I was the lone ranger on the precipice of suicide.

To avert loneliness, and to draw some needed attention, I went on a rant about cysts—that my brother called me his 'cyster,' though I was not nearly as prestigious as the *Sistine Chapel*. Hank, Finn and Henry and the other tourists were embarrassed by my digression.

"Did Mark Twain call his female siblings 'cysts'?" I asked the tour guide.

"Well, to my knowledge ..."

Cysts, clearly, were not known then, or if they were, no scientific data confirmed them.

"Be calm, would you," Hank said—his furry moustache emphasizing each word, as if he were Dr. Phil. "*Don't do the 'Agatha Show.' Just be you.*"

What does that mean—"*be you?*" Mathematically, a friend (who doesn't talk to me any more—I refused to pay for her meal at Tom's Diner in Manhattan) averred that: "You are what you are whenever you are being." To be, in whatever mood swing, is always to be you.

"Does this mean I can wear my Jersey Devil T-shirt?" I asked Hank.

"There is nothing controversial about the Jersey Devil," Uncle Henry said.

In Mark Twain's house, and for the duration of the visit, I didn't wear my T-shirt or throw any non-sequiturs in their drinks and remained as non-controversial as toilet paper. It was an insufferable weekend in which I embraced the C word: conventionality.

* * *

"Everyone succumbs to conventionality," my mother said when I dressed as the Hulk for a work Halloween party—using green food coloring, which nearly got me fired, because it spread all over the office IKEA furniture. Luckily, I stayed late, and with the help of Comet spray and a washcloth, removed it. There are still traces of green under the fluorescent lights.

* * *

I wanted to get run over by a car or stoned by residents of Jackson, Mississippi, for defending the rights of black citizens to use a whites-only water faucet. The ultimate self-murdering technique, however, was not important if I could rest with maggots in an imperial gravesite that my father promised me once I had my bat mitzvah.

"If you memorize your haftorah, I'll buy you this mini-tomb they have on sale," he said.

"Okay, Dad." I learned the Torah portion that suggests we humans are not bestial like animals because we have Judeo-Christian thought patterns that raise our moral standards.

* * *

I died the day Hank and Mother went on a cruise to Puerto Rico to celebrate his 2007 graduation.

I had found expired couscous in my fridge and snorted it.

Within hours, while Hank and Mother were drinking tequilas along the *Garita* at El Cañuelo in the San Juan Bay, I was dead.

* * *

It was a small funeral, and I was buried with two other dead people in the same mini-tomb. My co-dead people lost their composure ironing shirts for the local Little League team; they succumbed to heart attacks simultaneously.

As this was a Jewish burial (twenty-four hours and you go into the earth), and my mom and Hank did not think they'd be reimbursed for their cruise, Uncle Henry was the only one from that group in attendance.

Praying mantises were present—the talking ones who walk slickly on the coffin and dance in a mellow fashion while honors students upbraided me: "She hated herself because the Nobel Prize judges said her MFA was a vanity degree."

When no one looked, Uncle Henry put a copy of Franz Kafka's *The Trial* in my casket. It is still there, and likely will remain unread, because I don't have glasses down under. But thank you Uncle Henry—you cared enough.

AFTERNOON IN
THE LIVING ROOM

I WAS ALWAYS BROKE, ALTHOUGH I made $45,000 a year. I'd end up at my mom's house and she'd suggest that if I dust the furniture she'd give me ten dollars.

My mother was not home that afternoon and told my brother Harold to lend me ten dollars.

"Harold," I said, while dusting the hutch, "can you give me ten dollars?"

"I don't have ten dollars."

"Mommy said you would give it to me," I said while he waved his hand. Harold was always dismissive of me, particularly when it came to my financial matters.

Like most weeks, I was desperate, having spent my paycheck in a bar. I could make it through the week on gas and borrow my mom's tuna fish, peanut butter, rye bread—things she wouldn't miss because she's always food shopping.

* * *

My dad was sitting in his normal position on the rocking chair. He likes to catnap or peruse the *New York Times* and drink a cup of coffee. He had been getting weaker since chemotherapy and radiation, and the interferon made him nod off. He had renal carcinoma, which began in his kidneys and spread to the rest of his body. A balding man of seventy-five, he had scaly tumors on his head. Dad was pale and stretched out, with his feet on the ottoman. He had tufts of hair despite a bald spot. I called him Bozo and played with his hair, especially when he was sleeping. He'd wake up and say: "Agatha—stop that! I'm trying to sleep, damn it."

I annoyed and sometimes amused him, and this irked Harold.

Dad dug me because, like him, I was creative, whereas my siblings had more conventional pursuits such as elevator repair work or selling hotel toilets. He was thrilled at my poetry readings, which attracted boisterous plebeians in Izod shirts who believed that LBJ was more democratic than JFK. He even wrote a story about me as a Bohemian poet who lived with an unemployed viola player. Dad came to my readings to flirt with my friends as much as to listen; he especially loved *Allen Ginsberg Gets a Lobotomy*:

"You've cauterized your brain, Allen.
So, when will you end the human ego's war?
You don't feel because you have no brain left."

This poem annoyed Harold because Allen Ginsberg had once scoffed at Harold's question during an NYU reading.

"Was Baudelaire gay?" my brother asked the poet in front of several hundred audience members.

"We weren't that close," Ginsberg replied to much laughter.

Harold, who is more afraid of crowds than sex, never recovered from this public humiliation.

* * *

Like Dad, Harold had curly hair, and was also balding. Yet there was not one ounce of gray on his twenty-one-year-old head, whereas I, at twenty-four, resembled a young Susan Sontag. Still, I am not bald, although I am fat, but as I told Harold: "You can lose weight but you can't gain hair."

"Mommy said you have to give me money," I said, moving the

vases so I could dust under them. "You make money driving that ice cream truck—besides—you don't pay rent."

Harold resented that I reminded him of his employment, because he majored in philosophy at a local community college and was always on the Dean's List. The ice cream truck was temporary, he said, at least until law school.

"You're just a secretary, Agatha. You've got a bachelor's degree and you're taking steno for a Cambodian professor at Princeton … *big deal.*"

"I'm not leasing my life to Good Humor. And I can afford *my own* apartment." I nervously put photos back on the hutch.

Harold once made me so edgy I dropped Irish Belleek that had been my grandmother's.

"Agatha, why do you ask Mom for handouts?" Harold asked.

"I live on my own, Harold, and you pay what—thirty dollars a week in rent?"

"Mind your business, *slut!*"

"*Fuck you, Harold!*"

Dad was snoozing but heard us quarrelling. He sat up in his chair and looked at me. "Are you starting with your brother, Agatha?" His moustache was a thinning gray line that had once been fleshed out.

"Harold is supposed to give me ten dollars … *Mommy asked him to …*" I looked sternly at him, holding the dust rag. I was not supposed to use Lemon Pledge because Dad was allergic to it.

"The whore won't shut up!" Harold said, laughing. He had designer eyeglasses and bought expensive leather jackets that he subsequently returned after eight years and got his money back. He acquired fancy bookshelves and antiques from garage sales. My brother spent hours discussing his purchases with Daddy, who was impressed by Harold's sterling silver high school trophies, oil paintings by unknown artists and vanilla-smelling candles.

"You're such a faggot," I said. Harold, who is in the closet and meets men over the internet, doesn't admit he's gay. We were living in New Jersey in the nineties, and you didn't talk about that, at least not in Ocean County, which is also where the Hindenburg crashed.

"They hate fags here as much as they do in Alabama," I told my parents.

* * *

Harold lived with my mom and dad since high school and feigned "straight" for more than a decade. They knew he was queer but we didn't talk about it around company.

Harold, who abhors being called "faggot," grabbed me by my collar and pushed. I, in turn, screeched: "Blow job," and he pummeled me in the head. He was bashing me, while I scratched his chest. We looked like we were dancing.

* * *

Things were not always this screwed up between me and Harold.

I snuggled with him when he was ten and I was thirteen. I'd slide under his comforter, put my arms around him, and brush up against his hair and feel him breathing. Then I'd kiss him on the face, his soft skin against my lips. Sometimes I put my arm over his chest, and we'd lie there for a while, nestled in the stillness of the house.

I regularly went to Harold's room in the morning until he became reluctant. He'd kick and tell me to leave. Harold detested me so close and I began to dislike his voice—it sounded like gnats buzzing on a cow. As he got older, he became incredibly self-involved and completely unaffectionate. And he never stopped talking. He spoke like a helium balloon releasing a thousand dictionary entries. I bribed him not to speak at night because his sounds made me uncomfortable and prevented me from sleeping. Harold was enraged that I monitored his speech patterns. I have since made amends for shutting him up, but he has not let me kiss him—he barely shakes my hand.

* * *

My father, who tilted his head in our direction, tried to discern what we were doing, and said: "Stop it!"

Harold punched me in the head and I pressed my nails against him as a feline might toward an antagonistic dog in a midnight skirmish.

"She started it!"

Fudge packer! I howled, while Harold pushed me on the floor. It was a miracle the neighbors didn't call the cops, because our living room window is an expansive area of glass that overlooks the front yard.

"Stop it, damn it!" my father said. I was on the floor crying.

"Daddy, he owes me money."

"I'm not giving her anything."

"You always instigate, Agatha. *You know I'm not feeling well ...*"

"He called me a whore, Daddy, and I'm calling the police."

Fortunately, my mother was bringing in groceries. She was a small woman with brown hair and wore Harold's jackets.

"What happened, Agatha?"

"Harold won't give me the ten dollars. I thought you weren't coming home until this evening." I kept crying while my father offered me a tissue.

"Did you get the dusting done?"

"No, I didn't get the frigging dusting done 'cause your *faygelah* son beat the shit out of me."

"You're older than Harold ... you know better," Mom said, putting her packages down. She tried to soothe me as my head pounded. It must be this way for boxers who feel their heads aching, even days after the dude assaulting them is finished.

"Agatha scratched my chest ... she might have AIDS. I'm going to Dr. Lipton." Harold's hair was messed up, falling on top of his baldness.

My dad reprimanded him. "You shouldn't hit your sister."

"She started."

My father looked at him benignly.

"If you didn't open your big mouth," Dad said, mumbling in

my direction. He was breathing with difficulty, and my mom asked him if he was okay, despite the "slovenly behavior of his children."

"Harold, why don't you bring in the groceries?"

Mom went near my father and asked: "Do you want to go into your room, sweetie?" They walked together slowly, with Dad leaning against her.

WHY DADDY LEFT US

MY BROTHERS HAVE MET HER. She is apparently a likable person that my father sees when he doesn't see us. He tells us he is going to the homeless shelter or the zoo. Sometimes he travels in his station wagon.

My mother is dying of cancer. This is not a good time but she thinks we ought to realize that our daddy has eclipsed, over the years, with this other woman who likes my father because he is an intellectual man who is full of good ideas about writing.

My mother, I think, is implying that some women, particularly this woman, are attracted to men like my father who wear collegiate suits and discuss Hemingway excitedly.

My father's words are different than Jersey conversation, which divulges a dog's bladder has been diagnosed with cancer, or Richard Nixon's former housekeeper lives in Saddle River.

This woman took my father. She dispelled all theories about me and my mom and brothers and we are frightened of her.

My father died thirteen years ago and there was never any mention of this woman, and now that my mother has cancer, and will likely die, there are varying degrees of hints that float through our minds.

The girl in the next room. The woman who intrigues him. The daddy taken out of his station wagon while viewing *The Poseidon Adventure* with his kids—he is charmed by the sinews and styles and comfortable awes of this woman.

"Would you like to meet her?" my father asks me. He is burning tobacco in his pipe, the kind, his colleagues tell me, in their pock-marked faces, which destroyed him.

He is under the earth. In a warm-lined brown dirt area, sometimes where the trees line up, not far from Aunt Lillie's grave, where the weeds and stones meet for coffee.

Yes, Daddy persists, through the air, tepid and bitter, to have this woman in his time. The time he is not with us. The boxed windows where we look through and they are together.

"I don't want to meet your girlfriend," I say.

"Your brother met her. He liked her. You will get used to it—I have left Mom." He and this woman met while he was dead.

My mother has gone to join them, and it will be remarkably cold. It is not the maggots that will leave her pale.

My father and this female drink coffee.

"Daddy," I ask, "why?"

"Well," he says, looking at our bathroom tiles, "we discuss writing. She makes me smirk. I am content in her arms. We kiss well. Your mother and I have not spoken in thirteen years."

My mother was the superior lover in bed, yet she and Daddy are no longer here.

We are in a new house near a highway. I live with my brothers and stay in the bedroom and don't worry about God or fixtures on the wall or Daddy.

You thought he'd rescue you or put you to sleep in the back of your car or that someone would tell you how much he loved you. You didn't think there'd be empty boxes instead of his calming hands.

But the cemetery is quieter now. Mother has joined them for tea, and divorce proceedings are in the sand.

CONVERTS

WE GO TO FOGHORN'S, WHICH has the flag of Texas and is devoted to good steaks. There are frontier cowboys on its walls, and the manager comes up to our table and says, "Welcome to Foghorn's." He also gives us a free appetizer coupon we can use next time.

* * *

A week later, Bruce's girlfriend Christine says, "Your sister hit on the waitress at Foghorn's—it was really embarrassing!"

"Why did you do that, Agatha?" he asks me on the phone.

What the fuck is Christine talking about, I wonder.

* * *

This is how I see it:

We go to Foghorn's: my mother, Aunt Sherri, Bruce and his tobacco-breath paramour, Christine. We eat at a huge table and a blonde waitress named Maggie asks, "May I take your order?"

"I'd like whatever you're having," is my response. She has multi-colored buttons declaring the restaurant's specials.

The waitress politely grimaces.

Christine chimes in, "You look familiar. Did you go to Lakewood High?"

"I went to Jackson but my boyfriend is from Lakewood."

"Really?" Christine, who is ten years Bruce's senior (she insisted he buy a $1,000,000 life insurance policy she'd get) rolls her eyes at me and triumphantly acknowledges Maggie, our waitress. Maggie likely doesn't make enough money to sit in Christine's kitchen, but for now, her existence is a wondrous thing.

Maggie writes down our orders in messy handwriting, with the *b*'s and *t*'s interfacing with the vowels. When she's three meters away, I mumble, "Her behind is cuter than a pony's." My dinner mates are slightly shell-shocked because their world, that is, Central New Jersey, is not the West Village (even if Orthodox Jewish men cruise each other's reading material over Frappuccinos at the local Barnes & Noble café).

* * *

This is how Bruce (who sees everything through Christine's eyes) remembers it:

"Hey baby," I flirt, "my name is Agatha and I want to have your baby. Want to go on a date?"

Bruce and Christine stare disparagingly at me.

"That's completely sexist," says Christine, who five minutes before was grabbing my brother's three testicles. Christine recurrently informs us that Bruce has three testicles, and bitterly points out that it was "child abuse because your mother did not have one surgically removed!"

* * *

Aunt Sherri, who is in her sixties and is slightly more progressive than my mother, who is in her eighties, adds, "Agatha, you shouldn't even *whisper* those things to that waitress. It's awkward if she hears you."

The key word that any historian would cite is "*if.*"

* * *

Bruce insists I was acting like "a pimp over steaks."
"But Christine squeezed your balls at Foghorn's—" I say.
"You're a whore—" He hangs up.

* * *

I hope Bruce didn't really hang up.

I am holding a phone receiver in my childhood bedroom, where I grab a wrinkled hard copy of the *Village Voice* and look through its personal ads.

In the seventies, *The Voice* had the best male-to-male ads: men who like straight males, bi-males who want to bond over shish ke-bab, dudes who want to decorate their genitals with fruit before fellatio—all varieties in the *faygelah* sphere. Nowadays, classifieds are bland and most guys want to meet via Grindr while they are both at Subway chomping on a low-fat tuna hoagie.

* * *

When I was thirteen, I'd drool over my Walt Whitman's *Leaves of Grass*, reading, "I Sing the Body Electric."

"*Yowl!*" I'd greet "apprentice-boys" wrestling, their escapades in the countryside. I am enticed by the firemen's "muscle through clean-setting trousers" and their "waist-straps" bring me unfet-tered feelings in size twelve Wranglers.

I became less literary at sixteen and discovered the *Voice* ads, which, although they aren't as refined as Whitman, gave me quicker sparks. "Straight guys interested in having a one-night affair with a similar Joe" or "Bi-man would like to have an encounter with bi or married dude in the woods" are sexy.

I have since traversed through OkCupid where they have pho-tos of effeminate men in tight flowery undies and teddy bear dudes cuddling their hairy mates. Like Wikipedia, OkCupid is infinitely more expansive than *Encyclopedia Britannica*.

* * *

After Bruce hangs up, I realize that I am in New Jersey, having been fired recently from a job in North Carolina. I don't drive a car and Mother monopolizes the TV with her soap operas and cooking shows.

Life here is as happening as a spider breathing, so I go on my brother Harold's computer and Google some free men-on-men videos until I come to a site called "Converts to Gay" where men place personal ads seeking straight boys who'd like to experiment. The straight ones visit the "gay" apartments where they are filmed being seduced by the experienced gay boys. My friend Eric thinks "*all* these men are gay," that it's impossible to get "real guys who want to be fairies let alone videotape 'em."

"You can't fake this," I tell Eric, citing examples: a religious Jewish shipping clerk and Catholic lawyer commingle; a painter, who has a Tupperware business on the side, reaches a state of near bliss when he meets Franco, a muscled ex-porn star; Hank, who has seven children, has seconds of guilt but succumbs to one night with Friedrich.

Converts offers free video shots. The gratuitous videos induce me to do the "$4.95 Special" where you can see lengthier montages.

Johnny the construction worker visits Friedrich the Dutchman. Friedrich is the "converter."

"Hello, how are you? Come on in." Friedrich greets him, smiling at the camera and me.

"Fine," the construction worker nervously shakes hands with Friedrich. Friedrich is moderately muscular and has a receding blonde hairline.

"Cool," says Johnny, who wears tight denim and has a goatee. He looks like a hipster white boy.

"Do you mind if he films us?" Friedrich asks.

"No, that's cool." Friedrich sits next to Johnny, who folds his hands.

Every episode has the same apartment backdrop—a gray brick wall without photographs or posters.

Then the website closes the video. "If you want to see more, please sign up for a REAL CONVERSION for $45." I grab my credit card and return to the screen. It takes a minute for the movie to start again.

"Why don't you take off your clothes?" Friedrich says in a Dutch accent. He quickly helps Johnny take off his clothes. Friedrich grins at the straight man's muscles; it must be like this for Long Islanders who visit the Old City in Jerusalem, carrying the cross with their fellow Armenians—they find themselves in the crumbling rock tunnels during the Intifada.

"Yeah sure, dude, *no prob,*" is Johnny's response.

"You have nice arms," says Friedrich and he starts kissing Johnny.

Johnny and Friedrich are making out like those red plastic birds that repeatedly dipped themselves in water on my mother's windowsill in the seventies.

You see their bulging cucumbers. *I am in a state of euphoria...* and then my mother enters the room.

"Agatha, what are you doing?"

"Uh...*some research on the Internet, Mom,*" I look down at the computer screen, which shows two men exchanging spit.

"Aren't you ashamed of yourself?" she scolds me, her fifty-year-old. I wonder if she's going to put Ivory soap in my mouth. "At your age, and your mother catches you watching these vulgar—"

"It's a passing phase, Mom."

Besides, my brother Harold is gay, and "I'm going to share the costs with Harold."

"Hurry up, Agatha; I need you to vacuum." She's more angered by my domestic negligence than an aberrant sexual indulgence.

Despite Mother's continued naggings, I view five or six hours' worth: a tennis instructor meets a new partner, an unemployed deejay spends time without his chicks, a wannabe rapper humps Friedrich, a skinhead seduces Klaus (a German converter), and a construction worker gets a blow job.

* * *

When Harold comes home, he's furious, as Mother has informed him of my illicit activities. He contends the CIA might be unhappy with the porn site's cookies in his PC.

"You know I work for the government, Agatha!" Harold is a taxidermist in the wildlife section of a federal zoo. He stuffs dead coyotes and wolves, sewn by Jamaican ladies who are world renowned for this skill. Whenever he gets stopped by a police officer for speeding, which is not infrequent, he flashes his ID. He has not received a ticket yet.

"Would you like to split the fee, Harold?" My offer makes him angrier, although he meets men on the Internet, "but that's my business," he says.

"How much did it cost you?" Harold looks like some of the guys on the website.

"…only forty-five dollars…"

"You're not working, Agatha. Aren't you supposed to pay Mommy rent?" Harold puts his hand through his hair. He's already threatened to change the password so I won't have access to his computer.

* * *

"Hello," I call my therapist in North Carolina, "I've been watching X-rated gay male movies…"

"Are you lonely, Agatha?"

"I suppose." It's less fattening than the apple pie I devoured in my Charlotte, NC, apartment.

"You're setting yourself up for immediate rejection," he says in a hoarse voice. He is aware that I have no money, and we only speak if it's an emergency.

"Agatha, if you spent the forty-five dollars on therapy, it would be more rewarding." You can hear him *"tsking"* and tapping a pencil on his desk.

"Perhaps I can get a refund... I have a few days to cancel." I tell Dr. Marble that I'll call their customer service line.

"That would be fine," he says after I promise to phone him next Tuesday.

* * *

"Hello, this is Converts to Gay, may I have your credit card number, please?" a nasal voice asks.

"Hi...there..."

"May I help you, please?" The voice pauses to more silence.

"Hi there—*I er*—accidentally signed up for Converts to Gay." I wait a minute.

"What do you mean you *accidentally signed up*? How can you accidentally sign up?"

I do not respond to his question.

"Okay," he says, "what's your name?"

"Agatha Ravine..." He seems slightly startled, but nonplussed.

"Agatha, huh? Well, you're not the *first*. But is this—is this your first time with us?" He has little empathy and reacts as if I am getting arrested by the local police for entering his private property.

"Yeah." I sigh.

"Yeah, what—?"

"Look, sir," I say, hoping "sir" will not buttress his anger.

There is an interlude of five seconds that moves like nonstop traffic in Brooklyn.

"Okay," he speaks and my blood pressure rises, "here's your cancellation code—but don't do it again." He's like Bruce reprimanding me after lunch at Foghorn's.

I write down the number and praise Jesus as if this dude were the Lord, but before I can offer my extreme gratitude, he hangs up.

"Hello, anyone there?" No one answers, so I put the receiver down, not even jubilant about the money. I remember that the *Village Voice* is on the floor and a dog-eared copy of *Leaves of Grass* is under the bed.

MY MOTHER NEVER LIKED ME

I'M PRETTY SURE OF THAT. This was recently apparent when she refused to let me see my cousin Beth, whom I'm in love with, when we were staying in Toronto.

"Mom—she's in town."

"You are such a bitch!" Mom said. I had bitten her hand. I meant to gnaw, but the Labradoodle in me took over.

Mother wanted to see Beth and Beth's mom, Cousin Rhoda, alone; I was to remain in the hotel with my brother Oscar, who was incredibly hostile.

Oscar, who had recently turned black, announced, "We think your relationship with Beth is *Whitmanesque.*" He sat confidently, not noticing his new pigmentation was now comparable to our Hebrew brethren in Ethiopia.

* * *

My family is either on vacation in Brussels (where there's nothing to do but view the repetitious nature of the landscape), or at a holiday spot in Toronto, where we stay in our rooms.

* * *

Mother keeps me in a cave, like in *Plato's Republic*—a beast must always ensure the level between her head and the ceiling is an inch.

* * *

When Mommy was dying, Oscar got maddeningly impatient, and as I glanced over his shoulder, he screamed, "Get the fuck out of here!"

"Have you noticed that you are darker?" I said. He was giving Mom a morphine shot.

"Look slut, I'm going to crush you!" He echoed the feelings of other family members. I am what some might consider obnoxious and put ice down my grandmother's back. This procedure was not ignoble, because I did it after she had taken her heart medication.

Mom interceded on his behalf. "He's really a nice person." Her smile was fading in the cancer, and she wanted us to be happy.

* * *

On the way to work today, as it is Valentine's Day, I recall that my ex-girlfriend Emily declared I had Asperger's. [1]

"I saw this documentary on Channel 13 and you sound like it," she said. Emily had also written a paper about Asperger's syndrome at St. Germaine University and was convinced I was her cousin—the dude in Jerusalem who memorized polygamist texts from the Bible.

Emily is/was hot, so of course I told everyone, including a Pulitzer Prize-winning author who quit talking with me, that I had Asperger's syndrome. Emily, so sultry and persuasive, could have convinced a Koch brothers-funded think tank that it was a gasoline station.

I had known of Emily for forty-five years, but we had only spoken recently. She was a cheerleader in high school, whereas I was a protagonist in one of William Burroughs's heroin runs.

---

1 Emily refuses to believe Dr. Asperger was a Nazi doctor who sent his patients to Zyklon B showers. She also loves the sound of his name and refuses to consider that Asperger patients are merely part of the autism spectrum. "It takes away their uniqueness," she says.

* * *

My current psychiatrist, who is also my therapist, once studied autism in drosophilae. "You are definitely *not autistic*," he said. He had worked with fruit flies at Albert Einstein College of Medicine, and "your personality is more outgoing than the fruit fly."

* * *

Mother is overly anxious about me not suffocating Beth.

Her husband, my dad, was a writer, and she knew what it was like to find herself unexpectedly in a novel.

"Maybe a screenplay, Mom?"

"Leave Beth alone!" she says.

Mom also refuses to offend Beth's side of our family, the Kardashians, who vacation in California and pledge fraternities. We, the former papergirls and boys of Jersey, who delivered the *Asbury Park Press*, are forbidden to look at Beth. *But she is so gorgeous.*

* * *

When I first saw Beth, or noticed her, it was at her twin brothers' bar mitzvahs, which was like a wedding—three days of bounteous foods and fruits where Mother and her sister, Aunt Idie, made me feel as if I had caused the world to collapse.

"You are quite an ass," Aunt Idie, who sat at the head table, said. Aunt Idie once rode on a horse, at sixteen, and claimed she was better than my mother. She eventually married Uncle Michael, a one-armed owner of Hank's Chocolate & Cigarette Shop, which burned down in 1978.

Aunt Idie, sitting from her perch, rolled her eyes and said, "You must stop making our lives miserable!" She retreated to her fruit cup.

They were upset because I had asked their matronly aunt (under the pretext that I was completing a history project in human sexuality) about oral sex in the late 1890s.

Mother, also fearful I'd consume too many deviled eggs, reminded me, "You're gaining weight. Quit eating."

* * *

Cousin Beth was the smartest child in her family, said Uncle Michael, who died before he could carry on a conversation with her about "Ezra Pound receiving free room and board at St. Elizabeths Hospital," which, in 1855, had been established as the Government Hospital for the Insane in Washington, DC. Uncle Michael's favorite book had been *The Poetry of Ezra Pound* by Hugh Kenner, and he was equally addicted to listening to tapes of Pound on Mussolini's official radio station.

"She's the more intelligent one, the light bulb," acknowledged Uncle Michael, Aunt Idie's husband, who was not popular at family functions.

* * *

Beth read a poem at Aunt Idie's—*her grandmother's*—funeral.

"My Bubbie was there/when the water ceased/the sun didn't come/you were our heart…"

We gathered around the headstone, which was being unveiled.

"You weren't very nice to her, were you?" Beth said. That was the third time we'd ever spoken.

"Agatha broke her toilet seat," my brother Harold, who is gay but has a crush on Beth, said. He figured he'd inherit Aunt Idie's money because they both had curly hair, but then Beth and the twins came along.

* * *

Aunt Idie had nearly eviscerated me for smashing her porcelain toilet seat. She was equally incensed when I hitchhiked in Montreal. But the day of reckoning came when she slapped me because I blew air in her face.

"We didn't get on well," I told Beth.

"Certainly not," she said.

* * *

I am on the couch near Beth's mother, Rhoda, who is into art deco. She went from working in a china shop to owning art deco. I spent many hours in my youth with Rhoda, who dated men while I read comic books. Her dad, Uncle Michael, referred to her as "*Maydelah*," which, in Yiddish, means, "girl."

"*Come here, girl!*" he'd yell. Perhaps Rhoda felt that her Girl Friday status would be ameliorated if she married that flirty entrepreneurial dude who tripped over his shoelace in the china shop.

Beth smirks and sits between me and Rhoda. A being with black hair, she is a combination of her mother's brains and father's looks. We had never seen each other in adult form. I last saw her when she blew out candles and read the poem at Aunt Idie's unveiling. But to observe how alluring and intuitive she had become you'd never know it was that baby with green eyes with whom Uncle Michael wanted to carry on a conversation about modernist literature.

* * *

"You are just like Beth," her mother says.

"I'm getting a hysterectomy," I say.

"Only Beth can shock me," she says.

* * *

Beth came to my mother's house when things were falling apart. She was to attend grad school in New York and planned to hang out at Mom's in New Jersey. She didn't realize, through the bed covers, we'd face an exploding pancreas.

* * *

I instructed Beth to get off the bus in Lakewood. She said I told her Freehold.

"Lakewood," I said.

"You said *Freehold*," she said, giggling.

The Kardashian side of my family looks disdainfully at those who lead them to obscure New Jersey bus stops where Mexicans congregate for work. Not a place for social workers who may some- day get a trust find while observing famines in impoverished areas. If the trust funder/social worker has thoroughly embraced her burgeoning career, this will suffice until a man, skinnier than the Buddha, opens his Levi's. Indeed, Beth wishes to get married, like Rhoda, but lately has been rebelling toward independence.

* * *

Beth tried pussy with a woman who could have, should have been, Divine the drag queen/performer's understudy. Divine II's Facebook profile was a mere triangle, and when I met her in real life, I was astonished by her corpulence.

"She's big," I told Beth.

"I love her mind." Gorgeous women, and occasionally, very occasionally, gorgeous men like the brains of elephantine chicks. I have liked fat chicks, though never myself when I reach large proportions.

* * *

Heftiness did not compensate for her inability to be kind to Beth, and despite the profundity of their text messages, Divine II had sex with an alcoholic friend in Beth's grad school dorm room.

I tried to persuade Beth to evict them to a hotel, but Beth didn't want to be coldhearted.

"Your cousin Agatha is so cool," Divine II told Beth about me, and then I didn't want to intervene.

Thereafter Beth would say, in moments of anger, "You're like the pope during the Nazi invasion. You don't say shit."

* * *

Like me, Beth has stalked. She had a boyfriend who ignored her, even when they saw each other four years later at a hip bar.

"Want to buy me a drink?" she asked him.

He took his martini and left the stool. She cried until a canned-peach manufacturer offered to get her a Tequila Sunrise. This did not offset Beth's pain, because like me, we pursue malevolent ghosts.

Beth's boyfriend Charles is less innocuous than Emily, my ex, who calls me every six months and hangs up if she believes I'm over her. Then I begin anew: six more months of calling until I stop. It's been seven months since I received a hang up, and I wonder if she's lost interest in my potential to lose interest in her crucifixion techniques.

* * *

Before my mother died, I wanted to kiss her on the lips, even though I know she hates this. It sends a message loud and triumphant through the house that her daughter, the dyke, Agatha, wants to have sex with her mother. No, not true. I love my mom. Her voice in a saved voicemail makes me cry. I wanted to get her mad, have her evocative and provocative attitude shame me in front of my siblings, so we'd at least know she was alive. When she allowed me to kiss her on the lips, it was quite clear she was dying.

* * *

My mother is not a vampire, but they think I am, for kissing a near dead woman.

"You are horrible," our neighbor from across the street said. She's now a yoga instructor but occasionally reverts to self-righteousness.

* * *

On the death bed Beth gives my mom the shots.

"No," she yells at me, "stop that," as I lean against my mother's pillow. My mom is frail and sinking.

Beth ushers in the morphine, methodically, whereas I can barely get it from the refrigerator to the bedroom.

We gather around her bed. She discusses recipes. *Making pies with her mother.*

"This is how people die," says Oscar, who read up on death in hospice literature.

To me it makes perfect sense. When Dad was deteriorating, he could only discuss the Mets, not Karl Marx or the rise of Stalinism.

We sit and watch. A few breaths. Fewer. Impending silence.

The Colombian nurse touches her pulse and tells us it's over. She covers my mom with a sheet.

* * *

The day my mom dies we celebrate Beth's birthday. I get her a cheesecake, though her mother insists on paying for it.

We buy the cheesecake before Mom dies.

Beth has brown hair and green eyes and protruding lips. Her hands are quite tender. She can blow out a candle without effort.

* * *

When I rename Philip Roth's *Portnoy's Complaint*, "The Ejaculation Proclamation," everyone thinks I'm obsessed with sex.

* * *

Philip Roth may use semen in metaphors—call women "cunts" without even a euphemism to decry his vulgarity, but as a female and not a former valedictorian who has read all the works of Primo Levi, I must fit properly into a square.

* * *

Beth is a Jew girl who Philip Roth would date, at least for five minutes, before seeing her as some vigilant attempt to remain with Jews. To him she is just *a carpet muncher. Vagina. Ex-box licker.*

* * *

To me Beth is an illusion of some girl I'd date, like my ex.
Beth snickers on the phone.
She beleaguers my ex with insidious verbiage.
"Emily is a sick bitch who wants to get you started," Beth says.

* * *

My mom agreed with my brothers in keeping me under quarantine, particularly around the young relatives.

* * *

Mom and Aunt Idie were Beth's secret service. Now that they're dead, it is just her mom Rhoda who does the guard work.
Rhoda perches herself outside Beth's room when I call.
"She can't come to the phone, she's sick," Rhoda says, though I know Beth's been working at the mall for five hours.
Rhoda isn't as censorial as the elder ladies were—she's just omnipresent, or wants to be, like Zeus.

* * *

My mother had a crush on my brother Harold.
My cousin Rhoda has a crush on my cousin Jason.
My cousin Kurt, one of the twins, has a crush on Rhoda.
I have a crush on Beth, which they all seem to know.
My brother Harold, whom my mother had a crush on, asks

Beth, *"Would you date Agatha?"* Harold, who I also have a crush on, wants me to have a girlfriend.

* * *

"You and Agatha should become lovers," Harold says to Beth as he drives her to my mother's funeral.

"That's disgusting," she says, unable to get out of the car because Harold has the child lock on.

* * *

At night I sleep on the couch. My brother Oscar, who is six feet two and has a hard time sleeping on the couch, sleeps on my bed. Beth takes the chair next to me.

"Why are you doing this?" I ask her.

"What?"

"Sleeping next to me…"

"Because I love you."

I don't know what to say and she closes the curtain just like my mom, so the neighbors can't look in.

ONE SUMMER I WAS A MAID AT THE HYATT REGENCY

MOTHER SAID THERE'S NOTHING WRONG being a maid. My brothers, however, asked me if I'd put "housekeeper" on a resume.

It was my first job after college, and the maids who were employed for ten years or more couldn't comprehend why I got hired. For I was slower than camel dung in the sun, whereas these ladies were like metal balls in a pinball game—zip and zap and out of the room in forty-five minutes—the estimated time to clean a hotel suite.

I was reminded of the maid profession recently while staying at the Hilton in Secaucus, NJ. Things are well placed in a hotel room. This is the role of the housekeeper who must astutely put the retro ashtray close to the orange juice glasses. The bed is flat and the sheets are tucked with an anal-retentive zeal and complexity that only a housekeeper can muster. The smell of the room is antiseptic and reminiscent of dead bodies. Nothing moves but the dust. It is unlived in except for those few hours or weeks when people occupy temporary space. Apart from that, the life a room leads is largely with its housekeeper.

I was sometimes hung over when I got to work. No one noticed, especially my boss, whose name was Mayflower Jones. She was a blue-blood housekeeping supervisor whose father and mother grew up in Princeton. Mayflower received an MBA from Wharton.

When I showed Mayflower my resume, her main concern was: Have you ever cleaned toilets?

Mayflower was an urbane Aryan—the type I ultimately get a crush on. I get crushes on Mayflowers because they make me feel as if I'm a Charlotte Brontë heroine, who, upon meeting a Mayflower, has met Mr. Rochester.

Mayflower appreciated me more than the others—told me I was doing a "downright good job" while she stared more intensely at my uniform than most normal people who get a glimpse of the starched fabric and then move on to a more intriguing vision.

She was also amazed that I was an English major in college. I am usually more seasoned mentally than the people I work with. I have been a secretary for ConEd, a receptionist in a water-processing firm, and a computer-input assistant at the North Central Bronx Hospital. It's like being a whiz in remedial English class.

* * *

We assembled at six a.m. I wore white shoes (standard nurse ones) and picked shampoos. I was not the senior maid and waited until the others chose their supplies. You don't want to insult someone who has been there longer by grabbing the shampoos.

I took the vacuum on a cart and dragged everything to the elevator. I then faced a floor of unmade beds, cigarette buds mixed with room-service croissants, prophylactics, dental floss threads and occasionally, soiled Mary Higgins Clark novels.

I relished bathroom cleaning because of Comet's smell and its abrasive effects in shower stalls. I enjoy stretching my arm through a toilet bowl and using a brush to remove the excess dirt. I get satisfaction from a clean bowl—it looks like a birdbath when I'm done.

Beds are more complex and I hate hotel sheets—they are like pajamas for corpses. I placed them wrinkled under the comforter—for sheets do not have the virility of porcelain—toilets are the Spice Girls of cleaning.

Mayflower was extremely critical of my beds, for the pillow was off by several degrees, and although she would not fire me for messing it up, she gave me ten-minute lectures on sheet-folding etiquette.

She referred to me as the "The English Major" and took a special moment to tell the other maids, "Our Agatha here is an English major." Still, this did not preclude me from the same criticism that everyone else received.

"English Major," she yelled, "what smooth muscles you have!"

"Thanks, Mayflower."

"Would you like some corn relish?"

"No thanks, Mayflower." For she was our Mayflower Madam and we were her maids of suburbia.

Invariably, I could push that cart and go up and down the escalator with pizzazz, although not as exuberantly as the more senior staff.

Of course, all this was fine and dandy and dandy and fine and I never disliked being a maid until this girl from my Shakespeare 101 course asked me in the locker room, "You were an English major and now you're a maid?"

I looked at her and walked silently toward my cart.

Besides, I got D's in English and didn't want to be an English professor. My mother encouraged me to be some Ivy League thing, reminiscent of her wanting me to play the harp. Mom, however, was a bookkeeper, and quite good at it; but for me, well, she hoped I'd teach *The Faerie Queen* at Smith College.

While the Hyatt was not the Seven Sisters, it did have its merits. In fact, Mayflower selected some of us as winners of the "Summer Hyatt Maid Cleaning Contest."

One Jamaican woman was vehemently opposed to my nomination—she cleaned the chairman's penthouse suite. When she was sick one day, I broke her vacuum accidentally, and she thought I did it on purpose.

"You just a stupid white girl—what the hell you know about cleaning?!" said the elderly woman with grandchildren.

This did not dismay Mayflower because WASP-y women favor me. I'm like that Jew on the block who's quite clever. It's like having a pet you pay minimum wage to.

On the evening of the cleaning contest dinner, six of us ate in the Hyatt's exclusive restaurant on the third floor overlooking the town of Somerville, NJ.

Reaching for my filet mignon, I saw Mayflower gaze at me.

The conversations were separate, with Mayflower humoring me about some Stephen Spielberg movie while the other women buzzed like bees floating near lilacs.

When the room cleared, Mayflower said, "English Major, I've been thinking, how would you feel about a promotion?"

"Huh?"

"Would you like to be the new laundry room assistant? That way you could always be near my office."

I looked sad. She looked at me.

"Are you upset by this promotion?"

"Yeah, kind of."

"You'd be closer to my office."

"I know, but I just won this prize, and I actually enjoy cleaning toilets."

"You do?"

"I think it's refreshing to scrub them. It's a very pure act."

"Well, as you've won this award, I think it's time to move on."

"Yeah, I guess."

This meant no more trips through people's bedrooms as they were waking up, nor would it mean receiving a large tip from those I caught making love without a "Do Not Disturb" sign.

"*Enshüldigen Sie, bitte—*" I said, entering their room. I knew they were German because we had spoken the previous day about my having been an exchange student to Düsseldorf.

"*Ahhhhhhhhh!*" they shrieked in German.

An hour later, when I reentered the room, I found ten dollars in a silver tray.

"I wanted to be a maid," I said as Mayflower patted me on the back.

"You can still be a maid in spirit, but now you'll take care of everyone's dirty laundry." Mayflower thought she was very funny, but it was her good looks that allowed such jokes.

We were quiet for a moment.

"You have nice eyes," she said to me, "they remind me of zebra eyes. Did you ever look into their eyes? I notice on your resume that you were once a tour guide at the Great Adventure safari."

"Yes, I was once a maid, *er, uh,* tour guide." Mayflower moved her leg against mine.

"Did you enjoy that?" It was certainly less stressful than cleaning toilets but not the same money. Maids got more money than tour guides, but secretaries got the most.

"I enjoyed Great Adventure." I also enjoyed Mayflower near me.

"Would you like to come over to my apartment for a cup of coffee?"

"Sure."

Within minutes, Mayflower and I were walking. The town had a peculiar campus sensibility throughout. You knew there was a college nearby because of the university bus fumes.

"It's a humid night." She scrutinized me.

"Yeah," I said. I was itching from the uniform. Although I wore my own undergarments, the uniform made me feel like I was in the Prussian army.

"This is it." She looked at her door.

"I love the door," I said.

"Yeah," she said, motioning, "it's from Nancy, France."

"Nancy, France?"

"Oh yes, at the turn of the century, Nancy, France had the most art deco architecture anywhere. My father is an art historian and procures doors from France. This building was rebuilt by historical funds provided to my father for the restoration of architecture that resembles a Nancy, France, building."

How could a woman named Mayflower, whose father was obviously more than your average schoolteacher, be working as a supervisor in the housekeeping department at the Hyatt Regency? Perhaps that's why she hired me to work as a maid—she wanted me to rise in the hotel industry with her.

"So, you like being a maid?" She handed me a Michelob.

"It pays the bills. It's very serene."

"Yes," she sat close by, "so English Major, have you ever been with a girl before?"

"I have lots of girlfriends...I um..."

"Oh...you get around, huh?"

"I socialize with friends."

"But do you have a girlfriend?"

"No, none..."

"Would you like one?"

"Do you know anyone who is looking to have one?"

"*ME.*"

"Oh, you want to date me? Isn't that unethical being that you're my boss and all?"

Mayflower leaned over and kissed me.

"What are you doing?" I moved away.

"I couldn't resist your cuteness. Those zebra eyes...ever since you interviewed in my office..."

"Thanks, but I'm not really interested in women."

She got up and walked toward the window. It looked like a bay window you'd find in Brooklyn. I knew that because my grandmother lived in Brooklyn and called her window a bay window.

"My grandmother has a window like that—look, maybe I better leave." I eyed Mayflower who seemed distressed.

"Did I say something wrong?" she said.

"No."

"Then what's wrong?" she said.

"I've never been with a girl," I said.

"I can't hear you, Agatha."

"I've never been with a girl."

"Oh. I see. Just relax."

We lay there for several minutes and I began to unwind. You could see the moon descend through the window. It wasn't quite full, but it was getting there.

INHALING CALVIN KLEIN

I ASK HER FOR TIME TO consider us a possibility...there is always the possibility that it will be like a makeshift reality or a radial neck fracture when you fall in Rittenhouse Square after a lovely brunch. And it's not that you tripped on a rat, no, rats don't come out after two p.m., and they usually play at two a.m., when the humans are sleeping.

I want to be home sleeping with her—to kiss her neck and feel her breasts and let our arms just mingle/tingle. It would be nice if my dog were in the bathroom and her baby not screaming— yes, this is how I envision my Thomas More utopia, minus all the Protestants he killed.

It is then that I realize there is an interim.

Interims always and sometimes lack possibilities—like winning the Lotto at 7-Eleven.

She doesn't want to date an older woman, which I don't consider myself, but as she is forty-one and I'm fifty-four, this gap becomes a problem.

She lives in the suburbs, still with her ex-girlfriend, because they are trying to sell their house, though they have been together for fifteen years.

She approaches our conversations as if she is interviewing me for a job. Do you like children? Do you cook at home? What do you do for fun? Would you be able to send me a list of your ex-girlfriends?

A soul extraordinarily refined—she is an exhibit worth perusing at the Guggenheim Museum Bilbao along the Cantabrian Sea.

I do like them younger, the skin supple, and the face not wrecked from tense moments sitting on vinyl chairs at the cardiologist's.

A regular Madonna with infant in wedlock.

When I lived in Manhattan, my friends dubbed me the "*shiksa*[2] chaser," as I'd occasionally, and sometimes regularly, propose to Evangelicals with a Rolling Rock beer at a dyke bar along Hudson Street.

Since my mom's death, which will be three years this Sunday, I have found myself more attracted to moustached Jewish women.

Mother always made her preference known.

My brother's wife, who wanted to bury him in a Catholic cemetery, changed her decision after they discovered my sister-in-law had a tumor, which was then malignant, but subsequently benign, after they purchased new plots in our synagogue's graveyard.

My reticent/potential lover wants me to join her church. If I join her house of God, Mom's ghost will light it on fire and elderly ladies with red and black wigs will witness their hairpieces burn.

Mother is/was adamant about her kids not converting. Her father, whose soul does not rest, farted whenever they passed a cathedral in Montreal.

My mother, born in 1920, does not want me to marry a woman, but if it must be a woman, please, send the kids to Hebrew school. Let them get free Hershey bars with orange peels and complimentary tickets to see the Mets—a reward for their Junior Congregation attendance.

With my infatuate, there is something inherently depressing, particularly after she emails a Smiths video, which inspires me to choose between cyanide or drinking a bottle of Calvin Klein perfume. And although I met Calvin Klein on Centre Street after 9/11, I never wanted to drink his perfume.

Eventually she stops sending e-mails.

2   Derogatory Yiddish term for non-Jewish females.

It is clear we aren't going to be paramours on the Caspian Sea, that is, elope with poontang intentions rather than enter mahjong competitions at the Y.

I'm a puppy in the shelter, hoping this chick will be her new master.

Every time my computer beeps I imagine she has written back, that yes, she wants more than sibling rivalry.

She'd let me hold her at seven p.m. on a Friday night. Feed her spaghetti or give a back massage.

It's nice to be buddies. Chums are superb beings. But now and then I want to hear someone breathe next to me at one in the morning when South Philly is finally quiet and the crack addicts have crashed. Yes, I have a dream.

THE BOY WHO USED
THE CURLING IRON

M Y EX-GIRLFRIEND EMILY SPOKE TO me in a dream. She said I could be in the same room as her, that I could talk through other people, and allowed me three words.

* * *

When I told my niece Tammy that I had asked ten boys to my Senior Farewell, she giggled, as she had been to hers the previous night, solo.

"I was so set on going," I told her, "it was more important than getting into my brother's pot."

Tammy was not averse to being alone because she often heard Ellen Degeneres blathering on about bullying, gays and pit bulls.

* * *

After the Senior Farewell, we ended up at my ex-girlfriend Emily's house. I was friends with her brother Marvin, who was in the social outcast spectrum like me, sorta between "no one knows who you are" and "no one really gives a shit." He and I and our entourage snorted Peruvian cocaine manufactured in Jersey City, NJ, on his dining room table.

Marvin's sister Emily was snorkeling through obscure novels in her bedroom; she was a bleep, like it's bleeping on your radio in a thunderstorm but you can't hear it. The white ingredient was the storm; the bleep was Emily, the hot librarian. Who *coulda, woulda* been able to concentrate on Emily Brontë with Emily reordering books?

* * *

Senior year I asked several boys to the dance, including twin Filipino brothers, one who styled his hair with a curling iron.

In 1980, we didn't ask lesbian lovers to the prom. We wouldn't think, after getting Macy's or JC Penney dresses, that Ellen Degeneres could lead us, with a pack of depraved German shepherds, to gay liberation.

Ellen-like chicks were popular in my high school. Emily even flipped them over her shoulders during cheerleading practice; she was closeted, of course, and her closeted hormones bounced like Jiffy popcorn.

And Ellen D would not have spoken to me—there were too many zits on my face—she'd have needed a dermatologist to interpret.

I was the worm in the puddle that you stomped on during recess.

* * *

I've never been cool; at the dyke bar in 1988, the assorted ladies shunned me.

If it had been hip to be gay in 1976, a *faygelah* would have dumped a Slurpee on me.

* * *

I wanted a skinny dude for the Senior Farewell. No activist. No moustache. No sideburns coming down.

I'd shave my legs, use my brothers' shaving cream, 'cause in our family, things were tight. We had detergent for shampoo, and hand me downs from a Dix Hills, Long Island, cousin who dated Adam Ant. While Emily took ballet lessons in Manhattan and got drunk in an Irish pub with Bobby Sherman's niece, I took public school violin lessons and played kickball in the street.

* * *

The first boy I asked, Nicholas, hung up. Nicholas exchanged baseball cards with my brother Harold, and I bugged Harold for his number because (I lied) Nicholas told me he needed assistance with a book report on *Wuthering Heights*.

"Hi, Nicholas." I sounded like an Inuit grabbing for meat at our kitchen table.

"Yeah…"

"This is Agatha…uuhhhh…"

"*Why?*"

"Well…"

"Would you like to go the Senior Farewell, *I'm…*"

"*What's that, Mom?* Listen….my mom's calling me…gotta go." *Click.*

* * *

My second boy, Sammy Jones, was a porn star. A twink's desire. *Or my desire. Or both of ours.* No muscles. Sammy hung out at our house playing marbles with my sibling Harold, who also had a crush on him.

Sammy liked our roof because the pipes leaked; my father was more interested in writing fiction than his children or fixing pipes. This impressed Sammy whose father was a Nazi and a plumber.

Ten years later, against his parents' wishes, Sammy married fat-breasted Jew-girl Erica Horowitz at the Ramada Inn.

When Harold left their marbles game to pee, I quietly broached the Senior Farewell.

"Hi, Sammy."

"Hi, Agatha."

"Sammy?"

"Yes?"

"Would you like to go to Senior Farewell with me?"

In 1980, when dorky girls (these days they say I'm "intelligent") asked "borderline normal" boys to the Senior Farewell—long before Anderson Cooper made bullying or homosexuality acceptable topics—this was tantamount to committing social suicide. You must understand, it was hard enough for Sammy Jones to breathe in the cafeteria (he had no physique whatsoever), but to take Agatha Ravine to the Senior Farewell, well, no, even Anderson Cooper would not have prevailed with his entire CNN crew coming to our high school then.

Sammy, hearing my Senior Farewell invitation, glanced over at Harold. "—*Gotta go.*"

* * *

Six dudes later, including the paper route boy (who quit delivering for three weeks), a failed Eagle Scout (he lived two blocks away), and a guy selling Spirograph sets (his uncle shoplifted them), I got a date.

Roberto, one of the Filipino twins, the less macho one, the one who used the curling iron, agreed to go.

"You like my hair?" he asked.

"It's gorgeous," I said, trailing his words. I love effeminate dudes—can fall asleep listening to them. Roberto touched his curls—he spent hours playing with his sister's curling iron.

My mother had purchased a curling iron for me and I burned my shag haircut. I was never happy with my hair; only ecstatic when born-again Jackie Smith braided it like Bo Derek, which nearly caused a race riot in high school.

Roberto's brother, Roberto II, was more distant, but with Roberto, I knew that although he'd prefer to wear my dress, and I his suit, he'd come.

"Would you go with me to the Senior Farewell?"

"Okay," Roberto said.

A week later, he said, his mother and twin brother made him bow out.

* * *

Emily had the opposite problem. All the boys wanted her. She couldn't keep the young males away—they were ringing her pink Cinderella phone like it was the Jerry Lewis muscular dystrophy telethon.

I, on the other hand, would not have known what to do with penises, though my brother showed me his, and his friend Bert asked me to give him a blow job. When Emily broke up with me, she no longer sympathized with my revulsion toward "the Bert blow job invitation," and it was at this point that I knew, yes, she no longer loved me.

But alas, boys were not an army of ants crawling on my sidewalk. This was why the Senior Farewell challenge meant so much. It was comparable to applying to an Ivy League university. With my horrible SAT scores, I was going to get rejected, but there was no point in not applying for Roberto, Sammy Jones, sperm and Yale.

* * *

Perhaps I should devote some copy to my Emily. I didn't know her in high school. I knew *of her*. She was a waitress, like me, at the Blue Moon Pizzeria. She sued them for paying her $1.65 an hour. She hated that there were cockroaches on the floor, and that when she got home she smelled like greasy oil even though her mother bought her expensive perfume.

Emily was on the math team and in the reptile club. *She was stunning*. She had black hair, green eyes and bellbottoms. Her lips were so soft that when you kissed them, you kissed a million Maggie Thatchers during their first orgasm.

With boys, however, she didn't have orgasms, or the possibility of them, which is why she left our school a year early.

* * *

Back in the secondary school days, however, we did not converse—it was like a vacuum stuck between our ears, unless I saw her smile between lockers, but that usually turned into a smirk.

* * *

We eventually rambled in each other's brain like circuitous routes traveling undirected until she decided that my emotions were more in need of her than me. I'm like that sneaker hanging on the telephone line that looks inviting at first, but after five months is an eyesore—Emily had one of her blue-collar friends cut me down with hedge clippers.

* * *

We slept in each other's beds, with her cats and my Jack Russell, unperturbed by the other's odors, until we weren't sleeping, and then she slammed the phone down.

* * *

In high school, I was in a play as Thurber's Mrs. Walter Mitty, whereas Emily was student government VP with heightened estrogen levels near cheerleaders.

* * *

She read *The Jungle* seventy times. Jean-Paul Sartre as well, but in the evenings. Jane Eyre and Jane Austin inspired my panic disorders, whereas her choice was Sylvia Plath on an acid trip.

* * *

We never spoke. *Notttttttttta word.*

I had a crush on her brother Marvin. He was like lilacs or cherry blossoms. It was even rumored, by the more jealous of our outcast friends, that Marvin had sex with a female prostitute in the Goon Motel along Route 19.

But you know boys, they didn't see me. I was a cloud of nuclear dust that defense department auditors couldn't see. I sat on the tile floor with Roberto and his curls, while a stampede of students, including my brothers, walked by.

* * *

During the weekends at Great Adventure's safari park, the largest in North America, I was a tour guide, and met my Senior Farewell date. His name was Alexander, and with or without gaydar, or a large CB radio antenna attached to your nose, you knew he was a *mo. Faygelah. Pooftah.*

* * *

I don't know why Emily dated me. I have never been busted for shoplifting. Allen Ginsberg wouldn't let me interview him in person. My underwear is oftentimes not 100% cotton. Yet there she was, sleeping next to me. Her soft brown hair (dyed) and mine (grey) and my dog and her cats embracing us and me snoring. She told me how hot I was, that she would only leave me if I gained weight because it might cause a stroke, not that it would impair me cosmetically.

* * *

Emily was my love, the love of my life, center of the universe, Abraham's competition for the idols and God, and then she wasn't.

* * *

She deleted me. Just like that. *A blank screen.* She even called once, like she knew I had gotten over her for thirty seconds, but then we were back in business, the obsession business I call it, where I am hooked into dialing the number I seek not to memorize, or the drugs I seek not to do, which is quite similar to dialing the phone number.

* * *

But alas, let's return to Great Adventure and the safari park where I worked as a safari tour guide and meandered toward the gay man of my dreams. He had a lisp. You know that lisp that makes all queens like discos and all discos like queens, even in Queens? Well, yes, he sloppily pronounced his words with the expertise of a woman who didn't see a speech therapist in elementary school. He was handsome, although it was clear, clearer than the ocean is green, that he was a girl.

* * *

I met him while he swept rocks in Great Adventure. The economy was so good then, they paid people minimum wage to sweep rocks.

"Hi," I said to Alex, which is what I called him.

"Hi, Agatha," he read my nametag.

"I need a date for the Senior Farewell."

"Cool," he said, staring at a prematurely bald bus driver. Alex had a crush on this bus driver, but the transportation dude was into female ostriches, which is why he always asked for "the safari route."

"Alex?" I vied for his attention.

"Oh sure, Agatha," Alex said, "I'll be *yuh...happy to...*"

* * *

To prepare for the Senior Farewell, my mother took me to Steinbach. I was reluctant because I've never liked dresses. They are comparable to bras—I know they are there, and you need to wear them, but I didn't.

* * *

Alex phoned the afternoon before the Senior Farewell.

"Agatha, I don't feel like going."

This was not going to do.

"What?"

"I have to go…" *Click. Rotary phones did not permit my quick response.*

I called him back…*slowly. It was like bowling,* you must wait for the dial tone, like pins, to come back.

No answer.

I called again.

No answer.

I called an hour later.

His dad answered.

"Hello?" A deep-sounding male *who would not have friended Elton John in a man's bar or on Grindr,* answered.

"Hello?"

"This is Agatha Rav—"

"What?"

He lived in Jackson, NJ, which was a cross between Louisiana and Florida, the more deserted areas that alligators, not Long Islanders, trespassed.

I wasn't, however, calling to discuss my Hebrew origins, and whether he and his white supremacist friends approved. I was phoning to discuss his son, who was supposed to come to the Senior Farewell, for which my parents spent a hundred dollars on a dress at Steinbach in Brick, NJ.

"Alexander, *er uh*, Alex, he's supposed to come with me to the Senior Farewell…*he just canceled.*"

"Heeee did what—"

I couldn't tell if he was surprised that I was a girl or that his son promised he'd go to a prom *not as the girl.*

"He was taking me to the Senior Farewell…called an hour ago to cancel; it's tonight, and…"

"*That little shit*…I'm going to beat the crap out of him," and according to Alex, Mr. Alex beat his buttocks blue with a hanger Alex used to drip dry his towels in the shower.

"It hurt like hell," he said to me at the Farewell table.

"I'm really sorry," I said, grinning, glad Alex was not dead, but grateful his father had been the catalyst for my not staying home to watch Larry Hagman and Barbara Eden dry fuck in *I Dream of Jeannie.*

* * *

I was sixteen and am now fifty-one, and things have changed not too rapidly. I am no longer attracted to men who look like women and probably more so to women who look like me.

* * *

When Alex and I got to the dance, they couldn't discern the girl from the boy. Bert, who wanted me to give him a blowjob, said, "They thought you were hot, but were really impressed with him/her."

* * *

The popular kids took turns touring our table. The salad leaves, and the misfits who sat at my table chewing them, were not altogether redeeming. Some kids had artificial limbs, while others read Anne Sexton and smoked clove cigarettes with Comet during their suicidal moments.

* * *

Following the stare/dare and eat your salad dressing while the football players eek and geek and get repulsed by the zoo-like behavior of the most repulsive members of the human race, we took our wheelchairs and prosthetics to Marvin's house, where we snorted cocaine with said football players. Jersey City-manufactured Peruvian cocaine makes popularity as meaningless as it is on Facebook.

* * *

While we kids snorted, Emily—in her room—read and inhaled words from God. That's why they're such good friends and she attends those insufferable twelve-step meetings with the paranoid feeling that God may take back the wisdom he has implanted in her febrile brain. They are buds, apparently, Emily and the Lord, and according to my records, she will never abandon him for me. I have tried reading the Bible to get some exclusivity with her, but to no avail.

* * *

Last night I dreamt Emily dated my brothers.

"Your sister looks pregnant," she told them. I was mounting walls, killing silverfish, trying to comprehend how she could go from me to these Neanderthals. Of course, they were much cooler and didn't look pregnant.

My brother Harold, a swimming consultant, and Oscar, another sibling, were courting Emily. I was not a contender, nor permitted to speak with her. Kind of like: I am banned from her universe—I might as well be in the Sahara testing water-resistant fruit flies.

* * *

I dance in my head where Emily is not. She comes and goes, and on occasion, I visit her in a nightmare. But for real bliss, I recall how many boys I asked to the Senior Farewell, and how eventually, I got one, with blue buttocks, to take me.

FRIENDS OF
MRS. WILLIAM BURROUGHS

EMILY WANTS TO KISS ME in the shower while I'm using Dr. Bronner's soap.

Emily assists William Burroughs's wife to raise money for a retirement fund. It doesn't occur to Emily that Mrs. Burroughs has been shot in Mexico with an apple on her head.

I ask Emily to marry me.

She is with her family and the Burroughs fundraisers, who are friends with her sister, Christmas Eva.

Emily helps me get from A to B and tells her family, "My girl's got her shit together now."

God puts Emily's face in my heart. I strive to let it go, but Emily's better than all the *shiksas* I've dated.

"You're whoring around!" Emily says, and sees me running with other women, including a Jew/Italian from the Bronx who lives in Italy.

She leaves me a letter and pays for my food.

My brother Oscar, upon seeing her, says to Emily, "Don't plague my sister."

Emily's brother Marvin is semi-delighted to see me. He has frosted his hair since my outing Emily.

After I outed Emily, she wanted to throw me out of the car, but I persuaded her to instead purge my dead mother's cupboard of tuna fish cans. *Solid white.*

There is a cyst in her intestines, which nearly ruined my vacation.

I'm worried she might die without me.

I hold her during chemotherapy treatments and radiation oncology appointments.

Our friends say she doesn't ask about *me*—the lost dust particle in a Bugs Bunny set where he runs from Elmer Fudd.

PEAS AND CARROTS

WHEN I FIRST PLAYED SOCCER in the mountains and wrote a poem about peas and carrots, Wendy cheered me on.

She was the most beautiful girl at the Zionist seminar and didn't resemble a Zionist.

We met at a weekend seminar in the Catskills where crisp leaves fell and John the Baptist of Manhattan led us to the lake.

I looked at her.

She smelled like the lilacs in my mom's house, which the hospice staff brought.

I wanted to kiss her, but John the Baptist had an inability to shut the fuck up so we kept laughing at his jokes about radar machines.

When we got to our cabin, I wanted to climb in her bed, but instead offered her cheese doodles.

* * *

I dreamt last night that we slept together, never kissing, but embracing, after she was disappointed by her trip to Israel.

"The conditions were horrendous," she said while Mother's ghost leaned on my door. "Can I sleep with you?"

We lay there, close, and she said, "Why don't you come closer?" I meandered until we were making love without touching one another.

Then she called me, inexplicably, and asked me to be her

girlfriend. *Her lover.* I was astounded but pleased that it had not been a momentary lapse on her part.

* * *

This morning I woke up and read that she was married. She also received her doctoral degree in entomology from Heidelberg University. I wondered if, like me, she had a professor named Donald E. Sutherland who made her determine if a cockroach in a Petri dish was left-handed, right-handed or ambidextrous.

* * *

We had not spoken since I insulted her from a pay phone booth during college, six years after the soccer game.

"Is this Wendy Holtzman?"

"Yes, who is this?"

"Agatha Ravine…"

"Agatha Ravine?"

She didn't know me. "Remember the peas and carrots poem?"

She didn't.

"Zionist camp?"

"Were you there?"

"Of course, I was…do you have Alzheimer's?"

"What?"

This conversation occurred after I phoned a boy in my Arab-Israeli conflict course. He wore a yarmulke with "Phil" sewn on it. "Is this Phil?"

"Yes, who is this?"

"I'm Agatha Ravine, and I'm in love with you." It was one in the morning and I was utterly drunk, but this didn't preclude Phil from slamming the phone and ignoring me during a heated discussion on the Suez Crisis the following Wednesday.

I used state university pay phone booths to harass men and women, usually at Ivy League colleges. To proclaim loudly: I love you and if you want, I'll take a Greyhound to your dorm room. I even spoke with John Kennedy, Jr., at Brown, but have no interest in celebrities. I appreciate those with aristocratic origins who are not famous but talk with me regardless of my mother having been an office manager for an import firm of water fountains for chickens that were manufactured on a kibbutz near Tel Aviv.

Bringing nice prepositions to the pay phone, however, was not part of my charm back in the day. I could barely prevent anger from lurching through me like diabetes mellitus.

* * *

I have nightmares where Wendy Holtzman despises me. She owns an ad agency, and when I show up she calls security.

This is not the woman who cheered me on during soccer—*"Go, Ravine! Go!"*

I am standing on Madison Avenue, and there she is, president of the ad agency, who has not forgiven me for spitting mean proverbs.

"It completely ruined my day," she says while touching my breasts.

I rub her neck and hum to sleep.

* * *

My apartment is in my parents' home, though they are dead. They hover near the electric ceiling fan. Sometimes they get cut in midair and their translucent cells bleed.

I thought, oh my God, Wendy will never caress my breasts, but there she is a little overweight and dancing in my bed.

* * *

I didn't want Wendy to return to Israel. I wanted her to stay with me in NJ.

My mother, who is now a ghost, and peruses all the females I date, does not approve of Wendy. Nonetheless, I relax with Wendy and inhale her pristine odor in the Jersey swamps and bowling alleys.

*   *   *

I write her an amends letter via Facebook. They now charge one dollar, whereas in the old days, they'd never charge you a dollar for your amends letter.

Dear Wendy,

You were so humane in summer camp.

Remember how other girls traipsed over my ego whereas you sent unconditional love violets in my direction?

More than likely, you will recall how I contacted you at your Cornell dorm and released profanities that even Hugh Hefner wouldn't utter.

Your friend Yvette Clarkson, also sweet to me, gave me a stern look several years later when she saw me along Greenwich Avenue near a French bistro. She stared but meant to say, "You vilified my Wendy via her Cornell pay phone."

I am so sorry if I caused you any pain. While you counsel dispossessed fruit flies with your PhD, it is unlikely you will recall when I, the Zionist on the lower end of the rectal thermometer, insulted you. It was because you did not remember me.

In addition, we slept together last night, but my mother walked in on us, and as she's a ghost I hope you will forgive her.

*   *   *

Images of Yvette Clarkson giving me indigestion before I eat expensive French bistro food, and Wendy, president of the Wendy Ad Agency on Madison Avenue, frowning at me like I shot her father, who had not been a sheriff, do not permit me to send the email.

*   *   *

Wendy was a congenial Zionist. Most Zionists from our camp treated me like a homeless person entering a Long Island City, New York, horror movie set or an off-Broadway stage production about the bubonic plague.

Not that Palestinians were any kinder; a West Bank resident, reading my satire (over my shoulder on the Brooklyn subway) about bar mitzvah standards falling to an all-time low in Ramallah, nearly sliced my neck.

* * *

Wendy now resembles Jane Fonda, and you can tell—as with most Hebraic-WASP-y ladies from privileged backgrounds past fifty—her skin is molding. She doesn't have that youthful prima donna appearance of *deutsches* Mädchen marching in Heidelberg for the Führer. She's more a post–Jane Fonda, after she's undergone plastic surgery. Mind you, Wendy does not resemble a lioness the way Jocelyn Wildenstein does; there's just no allure—no fixed income look of *I will hump you till happiness bleats from you like a dead goat preparing for its sacrifice at the altar, pre-Jesus.*

* * *

As we are not on speaking terms, and she would only know I'm stalking her if I looked at her LinkedIn, I linger in the melancholic moments of last night's dream.

* * *

Mother never wanted me to have a girlfriend, even a Jewish one. She would certainly have tolerated a *shagitz,*[3] but not a *shiksa.* Too many Jews killed during World War II for her daughter to mount *goyishe*[4] girls. Like the Hasidim, my mother believed that

---

3 Derogatory Yiddish term for "non-Jewish males."
4 Derogatory Yiddish term for "non-Jew."

we should have babies to make up for the six million. Mom was deeply offended when I said, "You have grand dogs," though she'd regularly extend a "Good yontiff" to my Jack Russell.

* * *

Wendy does not appear on the internet, so I stare at her thirty-seven friends on Facebook. It's like we haven't been apart in years, and that green-eyed waif, who quickly kicked the ball and encouraged me to do the same, kisses me on the cheek. I rest in her arms and put the milk away.

THE UNINVITED BAR
MITZVAH GUEST

STANLEY K OWNS A SMALL radio shop on Forest Avenue in Lakewood.

I walk in, having not seen him in thirty years.

"Stanley!" I say. "How are you?!"

"For virtue of your smile, *here!*" He hands me a CB radio because "You are the most jovial customer to enter in two decades."

* * *

Stanley didn't always like me. In Hebrew school, I invited him to my bat mitzvah and put beautiful stamps on his onionskin paper invitation.

Stanley didn't come or ask me to his.

* * *

In the kosher section of ShopRite, I see Stanley's mother pushing her cart.

"Hi!" I wave.

Mrs. K, who is balding, thrusts her hand in my direction.

* * *

A year earlier Mrs. K introduced a distant cousin of hers, Dr. Harold K, Sr., who gave an anti-immigrant speech at our public library.

After the lecture, I asked Dr. K why his isolationist views were reminiscent of members of Congress in 1942.

Stanley's mother grinned in my direction.

* * *

Stanley's friend, Herbie G, purses his lips like he's drinking lemon juice. He is Stanley K's shadow before, during and after our discussion about the ten plagues in Hebrew school.

* * *

In 1973, Herbie laughed when I recited the Hebrew alphabet. He also called me "Salami," though my Hebrew name was "Shlomit."

* * *

In 2003, Herbie commutes on a bus from Manhattan to Lakewood and cold-shoulders me, like we are still in Hebrew school.

* * *

Herbie suspects I have a crush on Stanley, or perhaps I'm climbing the social ladder because Stanley's father owns a chocolate factory whereas my dad is a receptionist at the Shell station.

* * *

The class was astounded when Amy Q (whom everyone, including me, had a crush on) brought a gold necklace as a gift to my bat mitzvah.

"Why didn't you invite me?" she asked.

"I didn't think you'd come."

"Didn't you?"

"I don't know."

Amy gave me the present but didn't stay for the reception.

AMY Q AND THE
GOLD NECKLACE

THE CLASS IS ASTOUNDED WHEN Amy Q (whom everyone, including me, has a crush on) brings a gold necklace as a gift to my bat mitzvah.

"Why didn't you invite me?" she asks.

"I didn't think you'd come."

"Didn't you?"

"I don't know."

Amy gives me the present but doesn't stay for the reception.

* * *

I'm standing near the cantor; she's in one of the rows, waiting for me to sing. I don't have a great singing voice, but the cantor and rabbi are amazed at how I memorize Hebrew from a tape recorder.

* * *

There's no evidence that Amy is married, so we assume she is not getting married.

I've searched the Internet—she has no trial records, taxes or Ancestry.com statements.

"Amy?"

"Yes?"

"Remember me?"

"No, maybe, I think…"

She is not interested.

This makes little sense as she brought a necklace to my bat mitzvah forty years ago.

* * *

A friend visits my dilapidated apartment in 1988.

"How is Amy Q?"

"She's getting married."

They can tell I'm disappointed, but insist she is happy.

* * *

In Hebrew school, Stanley has a crush on Amy. I have a crush on Stanley because I don't want anyone to think I have a crush on Amy, though Amy knows.

* * *

Stanley has a funny voice, like he's getting his nose reconstructed.

* * *

When Amy and I meet, she is in another relationship, yet at twelve a.m., I ask why she isn't dating me.

* * *

Amy Q was engaged. She didn't get married. The boys assume she likes girls. The girls assume she didn't meet the right boy, or maybe the fucking thing didn't work out.

* * *

I've been to her room where it's post-Hebrew Hebrew school.
Stanley has not been invited.
There are other women.
I am not the designated one.
I have never been the designated one.

* * *

Amy doesn't phone back, or admit she likes girls, though her
brother is more out than a tree.

Amy Q has a crush on her brother who might kill me if I phone
her.

He designed stained glass windows before he became a cele-
brated architect in Washington.

Amy and her brother have freckles and black hair and when I
wear a dress, she waves.

Their father is my father's doctor but doesn't stop the cancer
from spreading.

"It would have been nice if your father had been more forth-
coming," I say.

Amy is sweet and muses over my words.

She recedes in the background, though I see her smirk.

* * *

We, all of us with crushes on Amy Q, don't know if she still
sprints. Perhaps she owns a dog. We would like to kiss her, but this
happens only in the movies.

BESTIALITY

I'VE SEEN A DOCUMENTARY ABOUT bestiality. One owner was completely mesmerized by his horse. A woman couldn't refrain from kissing her monkey. I read *The Last Picture Show* where people have sex with barn animals. *Some dudes are so emotionally transfixed by animals that they reach an epiphany in a petting zoo.*

This is not how Henry and I sleep: we rarely if ever use the same mattress, and he chews bones while I read Martin Amis.

Henry rests on my chest, and when I move over, he sleeps on my back. He moves when I move. He breathes when I breathe. It is like having a shadow with organic fibers.

Henry doesn't know what the hell to do, at eleven months, when the poodles downstairs hump him.

"He stands there while my Molly gets on top of him…has no clue what's going on," my landlord, who walks Henry during the day, said.

Henry has never had sex with another animal, so he mounts the poodles like he might a stepladder, more to see what's behind it than what's inside.

* * *

Women think that I'm an Evel Knievel dyke, but I am really a frightened slug who can't function without its shell. I don't have a shell, so the slugs are better off. Henry, too, needs to transport his body near mine without fear of the world undermining his paws.

70

This was recently evident when I dated Edith, who told me her name was Cassandra. I knew it was Edith from the start, because Cassandra would have had blow-dried feathered hair, whereas Edith's bangs covered her face like big question marks. She also wore a rubber hair clip on our first date, "Which took me more than two hours to choose from the rest of my barrettes."

Edith's legs were thick like the Queen's dogs. You know how Queen Elizabeth's corgis resemble ottoman legs? Well, this was Edith, when she was getting up, when she was sitting down.

* * *

We met in a sushi restaurant. She was forty-five minutes late. I don't normally get upset, but the sushi restaurant was about to close and I didn't want to swallow expensive tuna like a seal.

* * *

I am overly nice to waiters. This was not on Edith's agenda. She wanted me to sit with her ottoman legs, offer her a sea of sushi, as if she were Queen Elizabeth, but fifty years younger.

* * *

Edith likes me because I am Jewish and own a dog; to her this is an incongruous but delightful mix.

* * *

When she wants to extend our dining privileges by five hours at the sushi restaurant, I can barely muster another five minutes. I envision her flailing legs in an orgasm, and how it must be like to have sex with robust pygmies.

I knew that Edith occupied copious amounts of space but didn't expect that her willowy dress could make her seem like a hovering cloud about to rain.

As she ran into the restaurant, I jumped.

"Hi!" she said.

"Hi," I whispered, with dumpling juice dripping down my chin.

"What're you wearing?" she said.

"Lauren…"

"*I loooove Lauren.*" She sat down, awkwardly spooning her tuna with chop sticks before shaking my hand. "When I wear Lauren, it makes me want to *rape* myself." *Red Flag #1.*

* * *

Red Flag #2: We were riding in my car and Henry put his paw on the clutch and Edith threw it off and pushed Henry who nearly flew out the window. *"Uh oh,"* came Edith's response, *"doggie suicide."*

* * *

Sushi and Edith are new. They became friends recently, so every night, instead of swimming or using the elliptical, Edith gets sushi to go.

Whereas I've been eating sushi since seventh grade.

Though my mom preyed upon our guilt to remain kosher, she fed our second stomach sushi from a downtown restaurant that eventually closed for food poisoning.

* * *

Edith is recently Jewish—a convert, who was kicked out of her Park Avenue synagogue in Manhattan because her ex-girlfriend, who is now a law clerk on the Supreme Court, embezzled $200,000 of their funds. Edith had to return her wigs, plus all those esoteric recipes with kosher frog legs. *Red Flag #3, per my shrink, Dr. Edward Horowitz-Ortiz, of Hispanic-Jewish origins.*

* * *

Edith would never ask, "Do you have sex with your dogs?" She respects me, my mind, though most of the time she discusses herself, and how she survived the Bernhard Goetz shootings.

An Amish girl from Brooklyn, Edith withstood the 1984 train ride when Mr. Goetz randomly aimed his .38 caliber revolver at her.

"Bernie," as my friend Sasha calls him, went on a rampage against women on the A train.

"Don't you mean David Berkowitz?" my psychiatrist, Dr. Edward Horowitz-Ortiz, asked.

"No," I said, "David Berkowitz shot girls in parking lots; Bernie murdered them in a subway car."

Psychiatrists believe they know everything, including how to assign your short story character a moniker comparable to your ex-lover's and inadvertently indict yourself for libel. However, when it comes it *NY Post* headlines, I am far more knowledgeable.

* * *

When "Bernie" was making his way into the headlines, Edith was sitting alone on the subway. She had purchased Lauren perfume, and didn't want it to mix with the effluvium of neighboring homeless kids who might also beg for her McDonald's breakfast.

Edith flipped through the *Daily News* and felt a bullet come through her Coach blue purse, which had just hit the fashion world, which was why it had been so costly and unavailable at outlet stores. She was enraged, to say the least, because it cost approximately five hundred dollars retail; though, like a new car, once it goes past the door/parking lot, it is somewhat devalued. Still, the thought of purchasing another Coach bag was insufferable.

Since that tragic but fortuitous accident, Edith has been a speaker for the "International Bernie Goetz We Got Hit by That Motherfucker in a Subway Car." An excellent rhetorician who combines elevator music and R&B with words from *Vogue*, she spoke at Rittenhouse Square in Philadelphia on our first date.

Edith was also impressed with Cynthia Sanchez, the CEO of the "International Bernie Goetz We Got Hit by That Motherfucker in a Subway Car," because she told Edith "What great potential you have," while placing her hand on Edith's knees. This made me slightly jealous, knowing that career and coochie, even in non-profit organizations, mix.

Edith's organization drew sizable crowds, including former New York mayoral candidates whose careers were over because of widely publicized porn texting and were now selling hot dogs in Rittenhouse Square, where the rat population had grown significantly and was responsible for the theft of numerous hot dogs from ex–NYC mayoral candidates.

Since Edith joined this organization, their bylaws had expanded to include "men who might have dressed up as women on the subway that day."

Before making its momentous decision to admit males, however, Edith's institute (the International Bernie Goetz We Got Hit by That Motherfucker in a Subway Car) consulted Ayn Rand's ghost through a Ouija board.

"Should we let them in, Ms. Rand?" They moved the Ouija board piece, which was less expensive than hiring a consultant from Fox News.

"Of course you should!" Rand said. "But confirm *they are not Trotskyites*." Based upon Rand's recommendation, XY chromosomes, particularly those whose forefathers had also not been screened by The House Un-American Activities Committee (HUAC), were invited to join.

* * *

Edith lectured the thirty bushy-haired men and women, some of whom wore toupees like token-booth clerks, but the raucous crowd was oblivious to her. Not until her Ottoman Empress knees cracked loudly—like popcorn in your momma's microwave—did the audience simmer down.

* * *

After the speech, I kissed Edith in the Center City parking lot. She also let me touch her breasts.

It was then that we had a conversation about pubic hair.

"Do you want me to shave it off?" I asked.

"What?"

"My ex-girlfriend was not fond of it."

"I'm not fond of your ex-girlfriend," she said.

Edith despised my other friends if they stole minutes from me when she needed to discuss herself. One of my voicemails particularly annoyed her: "I'm having tea with a friend who's considering shock therapy. You're welcome to join us."

There was no response. Twelve hours passed and then Edith rang me.

"I must be your priority!" she shouted like an indignant soprano uninvited to eat oysters with Pavarotti in a Parisian restaurant.

* * *

We discussed our possible fourth date, in which she would return a belt that she busted after purchasing it at Lucky Brand Jeans. But Edith stopped calling, just like that, as if it were the end of a speech. To this day I am not sure if she was compensated for the poorly fitting belt.

* * *

I sent Edith a selfie of me standing in Chelsea, where gay Orthodox Jews in that hood didn't know that her ex-lover—*the embezzler turned Supreme Court clerk*—"took one thousand egg challahs from their former Upper East Side synagogue and sold them to a Korean deli on the corner."

I beseeched Edith, "Please give me another chance. I'll negate my ego for the sake of yours."

We had never gotten beyond the kiss in the parking garage, which was particularly frustrating to Edith, who usually has sex on the first date.

"Did you not hear that I like sex on the first date?" she said.

* * *

People tell me I have monologues, not dialogues. An Orthodox Jewish therapist once attempted to have "practice conversations," but he "fired" me as his patient after I said the Palestine Liberation Organization was a peaceful organization.

* * *

I waited impatiently for Edith's phone ringtone, which is the theme song from *Jeopardy!* Nothing but Republicans on talk radio was heard.

* * *

After I watched an episode of *Mad Men*—where the character Campbell has sex with an electric shock therapy patient, I realized it was never Edith or her buttocks or her jelly lips that riddled my insides. I just couldn't have what I didn't want. The termination of the club that temporarily wanted you as a member, suddenly, even that fucking club didn't want you.

THE VALUE OF OXYCODONE

OXYCODONE HAS A DIFFERENT STREET value per each pharmaceutical company.

I took my generic brand to the corner of Broad and Snyder, near the Walgreens, to an unfamiliar face who seemingly did drugs, and said, "I broke my shoulder."

"What?"

"I fell down the stairs like Dustin Hoffman—when he's walking down the stairs in *Tootsie* and reveals his male identity."

"Do you have fifty cents?" the stranger asked me.

"Can you let me finish?" I continued discussing my almost demise. "I broke my shoulder in three places and now have oxycodone. What do you think the generic value is worth?"

"You don't have fifty cents?"

"Do you know anyone who would be interested in buying this?" I pursued my unmitigated business transaction.

* * *

"*Hold on! Hold on!* You don't need to deliberate the price," a neighboring Walgreens consumer, who had been eavesdropping on our conversation, added, "you can simply bury your oxycodone in coffee grinds."

* * *

Once, when I had knee surgery, I asked someone to throw my Percocet pills in the garbage, though I originally wanted to throw them in the toilet, but the person who dumped them in the garbage said, "If you flush the pills, you will ruin the Philadelphia water system." The same people, usually, who complain about Percocet in the water, purchase filtered water.

* * *

The eavesdropper, who aggressively entered our conversation near Walgreens, also felt that flushing Percocet would ruin the water supply.

"Don't you have a conscience?" the interloper asked.

"The point is not that the water will be cleaner, but that Alice Cooper is an amazing golf player in Arizona," the presiding homeless beggar, whom I had asked about oxycodone drug sales, said to this intrusive individual.

"Huh?" I asked.

"Look, you may not like to listen to Alice screaming, right, on a seventies playlist on Spotify, but the motherfucker can play golf like no one else. That's what all the retired Jewish senior citizens who have asthma problems in Phoenix, Arizona, say. He is their hero."

It was also true that Alice Cooper's dog, after imbibing some of his owner's oxycodone, had eaten the family turtle.

"Crunch! Crunch! Crunch!" the homeless beggar said. "You could hear him chewing it for miles." He looked at me perplexed. "Didn't you know about the Cooper turtle getting crunched by the drug-induced dog?"

"No."

"Well, have you ever had snapping turtle soup in South Jersey?"

"No, but my dad did before he died of renal carcinoma. I'm not sure which was more disturbing," I said.

* * *

I had a true period of hell when I had knee surgery and oxycodone. It was just me and the oxycodone, and the only thing that would get me to sleep was Carly Simon, whom my friend Q, a marijuana grower in Taiwan, recommended for her soothing mediocrity.

For it was during the contemplative moments of independence from a complete lack of independence that I felt like a prisoner in a cubicle on Rikers Island. The oxycodone microbes inhabited my being, my moral status, and created an inability to watch the TV show *Breaking Bad*—not because it was about crystal meth, no, in fact, I think that the use of oxycodone strengthened my moral hygiene to the point where I was a Seventh-day Adventist with knee surgery playing Carly Simon.

The reason I couldn't watch *Breaking Bad* or other disturbing TV shows about drugs or chaos was because my mind and body, in their Percocet rituals, were falling into a physical kaleidoscope of hell-bent images dancing up a spiral staircase in my cerebrum and not permitting me to sleep. Serious system overload between the TV world and my world would have occurred.

The only one who considered this might be a problem was my brother Oscar. While sitting in his orthopedic surgeon's office—he had broken his toes during Halloween while behaving like a platypus—he saw several people who resembled William Burroughs popping oxycodone.

(Even my Aunt Sherri, Oscar noted, who was a beacon in the Zionist community of Mt. Laurel, NJ, had a Percocet addiction and needed Narcotics Anonymous to ameliorate this predicament.)

Thus, Oscar, upon seeing the William Burroughs clones in his orthopedic surgeon's office—and contemplating that these insipid creatures had transformed into bald eagle opioid addicts—said, "You must get off that shit."

"Huh?"

"You will turn into a bald eagle popping Life Savers."

This was a grueling situation, because I was staying at my friend's apartment—lined with oil-painted vaginas that resembled bad Georgia O'Keeffe flowers—during my post–knee surgery days because she had an elevator (I had a flight of stairs in my apartment building). I had been so mesmerized by the oil-painted vaginas that I licked them. This was no good for me or her paintings, which I believe were worth about four thousand dollars each.

Thankfully, there was an atheistic lady who visited Buddhist shrines—a friend of a friend who also lived in this building and made me Vietnamese food fresh—she volunteered to take the Percocet to the apartment building garbage can.

"Do you mind?" I asked.

"Certainly not," she said. After all, if she could teach at business school, which she did, and give instructions on how to get your MBA, a drug dumping was an easy task.

Without much hesitancy, then, I gave her the pills.

I watched her.

They were leaving me.

I will not be William Burroughs with a gun shooting pigeons.

I would not be among those tragic beings at the local NA meeting who claim to have returned to the sewer after having been to Park Avenue.

I would not put a dent in the erotic art market, though that had not been my intention when I began to hallucinate and make physical contact with those wannabe Georgia O'Keeffe flowers.

* * *

This time around, however—that is, the broken shoulder period of my life—everyone was brimming with a green conscience and thought it quite possible that someone would, on garbage day in South Philly, break through the generic plastic of my garbage bag and steal the pills.

"Coffee grinds," a young man, who resembled Richard Nixon in hairline structure only, said, "you must mix them with coffee grinds to prevent their illicit reuse."

I am, in fact, a coffee connoisseur, though I put Trader Joe's soymilk into my La Colombe brew, which some people consider sacrilegious—like the time I wore shorts to an Orthodox syna-gogue on the Upper West Side in New York on the Sabbath.

"You fat goy," a guy with a Giants yarmulke who worked at Merrill Lynch yelled, "why are you degrading the entire congrega-tion by displaying your thighs?" He was the same yarmulke guy who tried to kiss me while I escaped through the MTA turnstile.

* * *

It then became obvious to me who the homeless man in front of Walgreens—with this great knowledge about Alice Cooper's golf-ing skills—was.

It was Annelise Soot, who had been a professional hockey play-er's daughter in my hometown.

While she now resembled a blonde Abraham Lincoln, she was once a petite girl who sometimes ate raw garlic in the high school cafeteria but complained about the olfactory dispositions of her fel-low students.

She loathed me.

Annelise Soot never quite made "most popular" in high school though she did hang out with cheerleaders.

She was also an imposter, not a real honors student; she man-aged to be number six in a class of three hundred because she took easy courses that were not in the college prep category.

When we were in freshman biology class together, she ex-claimed, in front of several others, "You stink." My menstrual aroma, I think it was.

When I attended our high school reunion and consumed beers at the cash-only reunion bar, leaving tips after they gave me free drinks, she also said, "You smell."

She was the kind of girl who always recognized suspicious scents that were not in the category of formaldehyde or Burberry.

On Facebook she could be seen hiking up various mountains with her husband and six daughters, who took gymnastic lessons with a woman who resembled a hobbit. Together they looked like they were auditioning for a New Jersey version of *The Sound of Music*.

"Annelise," I said to her, "why are you panhandling at Walgreens?"

"I'm doing an undercover story for the *Philadelphia Inquirer*. We believe there is a correlation between homeless people and the theft of shopping carts from Walgreens. These shopping carts are very expensive, so we have volunteered to do an undercover story for Walgreens, and they, in turn, will take out a big advertisement in our Sunday paper, when we release the article."

"Stolen shopping carts, what?"

"We'll get to the bottom or the top of this. Crack addicts who steal them are not that subtle. What the fuck are you doing here?"

"I live in South Philly," I said, while she stared angrily through her Abe Lincoln blonde costume.

"I thought I left you in high school," she said under her breath.

* * *

Annelise Soot detested every cell in my neglected physique, but she bent her head now and then to speak with me about her accomplishments.

"I'm in Honor Society, are you?" she said over the high school cafeteria wooden table, where I had several weeks ago picked up a rubber, thinking it might be a broken balloon.

"My mother is a professional hockey player," Annelise continued, "isn't yours a bookkeeper at a company that imports anti-cellulite pills from North Korea?"

True, on most levels, she was indefatigably superior, except for her indulgence in garlic, which alienated her from the cheerleaders whom some of us suspected she had crushes on.

Annelise's mother, who was a professional hockey player, had beaten her husband with a hockey stick and he had jumped out of the bathroom window. He left the family.

This incident gave Annelise an inferiority complex as well as a lingering desire to smell other people—to see if there was an un-subtle and demeaning insecurity about them that was not obvious.

* * *

Annelise was prying the homeless in front of Walgreens for information about crack addicts who might have stolen the carts.

"Have you seen a crack addict pushing a cart?" she asked a Muslim woman who didn't appear to be homeless.

"Get the fuck out of my way," the lady in a hijab said.

"Excuse me?" Annelise was not used to folks throwing epithets her way.

"I said get the fuck *outta* my way." The woman led her children down the street like a momma bear and her cubs.

"Do you like your children hearing bad words?" Annelise said.

"Fuck you," the woman said. Her little darlings also screamed the F word in our direction.

"I tell you the world is going to shit," she said.

"Not like it was so great when we were in high school," I said.

"You were annoying then, and you are annoying now. Are you so desperate that you would panhandle oxycodone? What the hell is wrong with you?"

"I'm trying to purchase the complete collection of Primo Levi's works."

Annelise didn't know who Primo Levi was.

She took off her Abraham Lincoln blonde attire and resembled an older version of the younger girl who told me I smelled.

"Do I still smell?" I asked her.

"What?"

"You've often accused me of smelling."

"Look, you are as peculiar now as you were then."

She put her costume into a bag and waved down a cab.

There was no hint of garlic from her.

"Well, at least you don't still live in Lakewood with your mother."

"My mother is dead," I replied. My shoulder was beginning to bother me and I considered not selling the oxycodone.

The cab stopped for Annelise. "It's time for me to go. Good luck with your oxycodone sales." It was like the time she remarked that I wasn't in Honor Society.

* * *

That night I tried to use the oxycodone, but I had already mixed the pills with La Colombe coffee grinds. The Percocet was indistinguishable from the coffee debris and blurring in blue and no longer available for me to zigzag into a sphere of thought not my own.

MIDDLE

MY FATHER AND I TOUR Middle, where children and stepfathers and wives hurriedly exit from their beds.

My brother Harold lives in Middle, where people do not wish to live in the semi-rural area next to it. They prefer a suburban dog/cat infestation.

While we drive, we see a festival with freaks selling oranges and Captain Jack T-shirts. The freaks two-faced ladies, hypocritical pornographers, astute stamp collectors, Indonesian spelling bee winners, infrared gamma ray strip teasers who are currently unemployed—say, "You can do your laundry here."

Into their machine I throw my purse, vitamin C pills, and leftover Prozac, which was canceled after my therapist said I wasn't depressed. The credit cards melt. The dollar bills get soaked. The pills dissolve.

* * *

To thank my hosts, I make pasta with Italian cheeses though the spaghetti mixes with laundry detergent.

Anyone who eats the pasta tastes soap and salt and salt and soap and crystals in the pasta.

* * *

I see wiry women in a wall-paneled room that resembles my seventies basement.

These ladies work for a person called "Overseer."

An XX chromosomal being with green lipstick flirts with me. "You are so darling." She kisses my cheek, rubbing her nails on my face.

Another person blows bubbles at me. This creature, the bubble lady, lets me sleep with her.

These girls dislike their "Overseer."

They are, however, mesmerized by my soapsuds; they don't know inattentive types who make lasagna with Tide.

* * *

Middle people are not distracted. They are owners of depraved ferrets imprisoned in New Zealand Maybelline factories and rescued by PETA activists. Others belong to the National Liberation for the Establishment of People Who Were Evicted from Elementary School Because of Impetigo.

They are appalled and fascinated, but never absentminded.

* * *

My father is on tour in Middle, where my brother Harold lives. Everyone likes my father who is only angry with his children, not the public, and is a liberal who despises Republican coworkers.

Daddy grins, doesn't denounce others, except if you are a narcissistic Right to Life president—then he loses his mind; indeed, you will not receive his cherished Franklin D. Roosevelt smirk.

* * *

One damsel gives me a yellow-lined piece of paper, which delineates why she and her colleagues loathe their supervisor:

1. She discriminates against us when we menstruate
2. She likes boys more than men and is completely indifferent to us
3. Her knowledge of labor laws is nonexistent
4. We hope to place her body in the refrigerator

I put the yellow-lined paper into Gogol's *Dead Souls*. I travel with books and papers because I rarely lose the book, though I do lose the paper, but not if it's in the book.

Their boss sits me down.

"That's quite revolting," she says, laughing with sauce and suds on her lips.

"It was an accident."

I look for my dad who is taking me home, though I am fifty-three.

"What are you looking for?"

"My father."

"He's an agreeable man."

"Not if you like Richard Nixon."

I have been at this carnival too long.

Dad might leave without me. *I'm always somewhere while my dad is elsewhere and I forget about his role as car driver and he occasionally forgets me.*

"My brother Harold will pick me up," I say.

"What is that yellow-lined paper in your Gogol book?"

"Disparaging remarks about you."

"Huh?"

"The girls collaborated." I hand it to her.

Minutes later Harold comes.

The girls sneer, but soon it will be despair, not spaghetti and bubbles, that ruins their evening.

HOT CHOCOLATE IN
THE CUPBOARD

THE WORLD IS COMING TO an end, and an impoverished black woman, one of many people dispossessed by a shift in the equator, brings me spaghetti.

We want to cook it in the microwave oven, so I offer to share it with her; she declines; no, I insist, let's share, particularly during Black History Month (when liberals are plagued with more guilt than usual), but my brother objects. He claims she stole it from him.

He is putting pasta into the microwave while the rest of the world is starving. The rest of the world, that is, we who are living in one building, in which he is among the few who has pasta, sauces and Parmesan cheese.

"Does it really matter if the black woman and I eat this spaghetti?"

"She stole it from me," he says, and takes it from us, this food that doesn't exist elsewhere.

My brother is also not concerned that my dog is gone, missing, and no matter how many times I call her, she doesn't return.

I am quite lost without the dog, whether she is missing from the dorm or roaming highways. I think I'm going to see her again, but there is a slight chance she will not return because the pit bull venue is larger than it's been in previous years.

"Michael Vick just got caught," my friends assure me.

"And they steal dogs for this reason?"

Yes, even as the world is ending, and the black woman offers me Parmesan cheese that belongs to my brother's allotment, the dogs are fighting.

I once found my dog, but wasn't sure it was her, because they all look the same, particularly as the world is ending.

I look in the kitchen for my dog and food. There are only clothes and blankets and some hot chocolate, but the dust has ruined the materials we might wear, if it gets cold.

Most people have already stolen food, likely after the dust ravaged the organic nature of these products. That's why the cupboards are bare, minus the hot chocolate mix and clothes for the winter.

I am too intimidated to steal from the cabinets and should never have let my dog wander off.

Amid blank tables, the black lady and I hold hands and wait for God.

EXTENSION 501

I PHONED EACH TIME A THOUGHT arose.

He couldn't discern who it was, the owner or me, and every time he'd be in a meeting or the middle of a profound thought to save the company thousands of dollars, I'd be on the line. He didn't appreciate my calling because he's the boss and since the workforce is dependent on his discretionary skills and whether there will be a profit, he is our company's maintenance fee, you might say, after we sell the apartment.

My obsessive nature, in which I bother him with inanities like there are currently bagels in the kitchen, is debilitating, and his eyes get larger with each second that is stolen.

But more than the bagel digression, he is disturbed that his extension is burned into my head like Harry Potter's scar or Damien's 666.

When I'm done speaking with him, I feel like I've walked over a crate of broken eggs and shells and the yolk of my suffering is all over my leather high-heeled shoes, which I hope he noticed, since I normally wear sneakers and khaki pants with a men's button-up shirt.

At one point he charged me an interruption fee. I knew this was humorous, to some extent, and he, too, knew this was humorous, and I tried to subjugate this bad quality of mine, this definitely unprofessional habit, of interrupting him.

But alas, I was not able to fulfill my end of the bargain, that is, of not bothering him during a pragmatic discussion about avoiding environmental fees because we pollute the lake quite a bit.

Most people would be happy not to speak to their bosses.

Not me, I have tears coming down my face.

I remember the first time I left that company, or should I say the first time I left him, I was crying at the French Roast, this café along Sixth Avenue.

People do not understand why I commute from New York City to Greenwich, Connecticut, to work in a plastics factory. They cannot comprehend what is so fundamentally challenging about working with provincial Yankees and editing their ads.

I have a need to see him. To feel the paranoia go *boing! Boing!* To get scared when he's mad. To continuously ask, "Will I get fired?"

People trek in the Himalayas realizing the life-threatening problems involved. I climb all over his neurological freeways with similar risks.

I have been told to leave, for example, when I eat chocolate because it makes me hyper.

I have been told to leave when I drink coffee because it makes me boundless.

Yet he misses me or wants to take a walk in the rural parts of the town.

But then he tells me to get the fuck out of his office.

The other day I knew he was in a volatile mood.

He gets in a volatile mood when he's on the phone with his girl-friend who is an investment banker for the Catholic Church.

Since they are so similar, I don't understand how they achieve orgasm.

Most people need a yin or yang to cause a bang. With them it's like Businessperson 1.2 and Businessperson 1.3 and they could have met on Amtrak and decided to get married, which they did.

So, after he got off the phone with his insignificant other, as he sometimes refers to his housemate, he was in an extraordinarily bad mood.

He kept knocking things off his desk.

You could hear the paper clips falling all the way down the hall.

I kept calling extension 501.

He kept hanging up on me.

"Don't you want to hear how I found a major typo in the plastics ad in the *Times* before it went to print?"

"No!" Slam.

"I was able to save us a late fee on the printer charges—over three hundred dollars!"

"I'm in a meeting—*don't call me...*"

"Are you sure?"

Finally, not being able to stand my voice or intrusive nature or neediness, which leads to him yelling at me and me complaining about him yelling at me and him telling me how he doesn't want to hurt my feelings, to avoid all complexities that normally wouldn't bog down a VP, he said, "I don't want you to call me in the office..."

"What?" You could hear the crackles in my voice, like sparkles that have a few sparks left to sparkle.

"Why must you always invent new rules?"

"Because you create new problems..."

"I don't know what I'm going to do..." A silence of four minutes. "If I can't call you, doesn't that mean you shouldn't call me?"

"No, I'm your boss...and I don't interrupt you the way you interrupt me...I restrain myself..."

"So, you're saying..."

"I have to go."

Before I left that evening, I went by his office.

Both of us had a heavy red on our faces, like we might cry, equally upset by the other person's behavior.

"Good night."

"Yes, good night."

I went home and thought about other forms of communication that might enable me to apologize.

I could send him thoughts in an envelope.

"You inspire violet rays that rise from the fumes in our plastics factory." *Fifty cents and into the mailbox.*

"You are endearing like my blue-haired kindergarten teacher." *Fifty cents plus an additional twenty-one cents because that's a heavier thought.*

I considered sending an apologetic e-mail, "It's not my fault that I cause you distress."

Of course, no one wants to allude to the truth. Mystery is always a good way to avoid reality, especially if you love your boss who just assumes you are psychotic but in the back of his mind is completely aware of the reality that impedes normal behavior in the office.

Considering the bad economy, I pray a great deal more than usual, you know, to keep my job.

I stopped seeing my therapist because he falls asleep. Avoiding him I needed my boss. But he has too many budgetary concerns to discuss the Jungian origins of the *memememememememememememe complex* and how it manifests in the office.

To terminate telephone usage, I pasted my hand to the desk with Krazy Glue; put a dead cockroach on the receiver; spray-painted over the numbers "5," "0" and "1"; but the stalking sensations drove me to the wires.

I cannot avoid this instrument or the power of immediacy it gives me.

In seventh grade my brother Harold painted a picture of me with the phone attached to my head. These days it's an iPad connected to my esophagus.

Maybe if Alexander Graham Bell had been unsuccessful, the pounding sensations I receive when calling extension 501 would never have materialized.

As the BBC Radio transmits information on the Malayan capture of a Muslim initiating a rebellion in the Philippines, as the world collapses and the pitter patter nature of the rain encompasses a sky, I hope that a smile will reappear on his face by Monday.

MY DEAD GRANDMOTHER
AT THE MOVIES

M Y FRIEND BONNIE HAS NEVER left me, at least in the dream sequence where her face appears quite regularly.

Last night I brought my dead grandmother to the movie theater where Bonnie still works. Either Bonnie can't get a new job or she's stuck in my dreams. I can't determine if it's my unconscious psyche or the employment situation in New York, which is not supposed to be very good, at least not as good as where my brother Bruce lives—in Ohio.

I walk into the movie theater with the intention of seeing Bonnie and her roommate, Kim, who I'm also intrigued with; in this nightmare I am accompanied by my comatose grandmother. I have never had a crush on my grandmother and she doesn't resemble a corpse or a computer error, but there she is with her arm placed around mine. It's been like this for some time: when Ida, my grandmother, was alive, I'd walk her from her apartment to our car where my father was waiting. It was one of the greatest rituals of my lifetime, in addition to making Grandma instant coffee or putting pot roast in the oven for my mother. They both praised my cooking talents, but instant coffee and pot roast were not difficult; when you're doing it at sixteen, it's considered talent, particularly in Jersey, where being domestic was/is/can be prestigious.

And so my grandmother, who weighs less than half of me, walks with me into the film theater. We are seeing Bertolucci's *The*

Conformist, and though Grandma does not like movies because of her cataracts, she likes to hang out with me.

Bertolucci's movie, I am told, is about fascism. I have never seen it, but figure it is a good movie to take one's dead grandmother to. I also believe this date will make Bonnie jealous, though Bonnie recently shaved her head and looks like an Auschwitz victim and it is doubtful anyone else is crushing on her.

"Why did you shave your head?" I ask. "To be like that girl in the movie *Go Fish*?"

"Don't know what you're talking about," she says. She likes to be curt, and more importantly, doesn't like to know what I'm talking about.

"Have you met my grandmother?"

"Who?"

"This is Ida, my dead grandmother—we're going to the Bertolucci movie."

"Would you like something?" She is presiding over the popcorn counter.

"Are you going to acknowledge my deceased grandmother?"

"I don't see anyone."

I had heard, prior to this conversation, that Bonnie and her roommate, Kim, who also works here, decided I was too intense.

"I'd like some intense tea. Very intense. Do you like intensity?"

"We're totally intense," Kim, who is behind the popcorn counter, says.

"How many cents?" my grandmother asks. My grandmother, though she has been dead for ten years, is still concerned about money. Like my father, she grew up during the Depression, and it's not something you easily recover from.

"No, Grandma, it's okay, I got this. Do you want tea?"

"I'd like Sanka."

"Do you people have Sanka?" I look at Bonnie, and she looks at Kim, and they are both offended by this question.

"We have espresso or cappuccino or herbal tea."

"Grandma, would you like some cappuccino or espresso?"

"I don't know what they are." Grandma, who died in 1979,

never tasted cappuccino. It was not prominent in Ocean County, New Jersey, and even if it were, it is doubtful Grandma would have gone to the mall to drink it. To her coffee was coffee, and Sanka was the best of all of it. In fact, she loved the way I made it—mixing powdered cream with the black sprinkles. It was mesmerizing when the hot water mixed with the crystals and crackled and you smelled it. It was much easier than what Bonnie was doing.

"Maybe tea, Grandma?"

She nods.

"Would you please make my dead grandmother some tea?"

"What kind?" Bonnie says. Her grin is her first sign of warmth.

"Spearmint," I say.

She pouts. Twice in five minutes.

"Peppermint?" She blushes. The red looks lovely on her.

"Yeah." I don't know spearmint from peppermint—they all seem the same.

My grandmother grabs the cup. In Heaven, she regained some of her eyesight and dexterity, but is still bothered by cataracts.

I look at Bonnie and Kim as we enter the Bertolucci movie. Their friend Andrew lets us in gratis. I am famous for being infatuated with female ushers, and it is therefore acceptable to let me in—whereas Quentin Crisp and Spike Lee get in free because of their cinematic fame.

"Thanks." I wink at the girls because they've given me the drinks at no charge and I leave money in their tip cup.

"You're welcome," Bonnie says, snickering at Kim behind the counter.

It is the first time a dead grandmother has entered the movie theater with an infatuated, Sapphic relative, and indeed, it is the first time a customer has so distracted the employees' attention since Suzanne Vega came to the theater in a blue dress. Indeed, it takes a great deal to impress them, and while watching the Bertolucci movie, I turn to Grandma to see if she is there, but she has gone, sort of faded from the theater like Bonnie's lips and Bertolucci's goddess.

THE JEW WHO BECAME A NUN

MY EX-GIRLFRIEND EMILY DECLARED TO several people in our immediate social circle that I have multiple personalities. But it is Emily, I would argue, who has a diverse set of identities that bind to no particular individuality.

I'm not referring to her screaming unclear thoughts at the Pakistani cashier at 7-Eleven, or the time she refused to tip our waitress at Beefsteak Charlie's because her filet mignon was not quite 87°F.

No, it all began when Emily broke her brain running down the stairs of the Empire State Building; from that point onward, she spoke in cantankerous and garbled speeches that occasionally reeked of Goebbels on a bad day of PR.

* * *

"Disneyland! Disneyland!" Emily shouts while my friend Esther is on the phone planning a trip, having just learned her uncle died.

"Emily, shut up—stop screaming into your cell phone while I'm talking."

"We should go to Disneyland, *not South Dakota*, Esther."

"You're not coming regardless…"

"South Dakota attracts manic depressives, I read in *Vogue*."

Esther continues speaking with the travel agency.

Emily sings the theme song from *The Brady Bunch*, which is

her national anthem. She is particularly mesmerized by the episode where Jan uses lemon rinds to get rid of freckles.

Emily speaks, and never shuts up, and drowns out the looniest cartoon character. Her voice travels at quantum liquid spin speed—one light year from my house to yours, in thirty seconds of immense insects flying.

* * *

Though falling down the steps of the Empire State Building was a significant moment for Emily's unparalleled mental health issues, her descent into a Dante's *Inferno* of dementia began when she became a nun at Sister Jewniversity.

Emily was studying to become an endocrinologist's assistant at Sister Jewniversity while I went there to research Renaissance history—how the Vatican had scorned Catholics and Protestants pre- and post-Reformation.

We met at the latrine in the library between the Renaissance and endocrinologist sections.

"Hi," she said to me.

"Hi," I said.

We had been checking each other out between notes. Though it was clear that I liked her and she liked me, I was fixated on the Renaissance era but couldn't complete my paper.

To avert writer's block à la Renaissance, I decided to hitchhike to Connecticut. This journeying off might have led some to believe *that I had multiple personalities split between the Garden State Parkway and the Renaissance era.* Truth was: I was disappointed by the limited supply of Renaissance history books at Sister Jewniversity Library. I also couldn't write more about the Catholics and Protestants, who were getting on my nerves, so I traveled to Connecticut, under the severe impression I was going to marry a WASP (I'd never met) who'd have more resources about the Renaissance era than the library at Sister Jewniversity.

* * *

Sister Jewniversity has historically been a bastion of anti-Semitic–anti-Zionist lesbianism directed at the ultra-Orthodox queer female Jews who live in the same neighborhood and drive improperly when it is not Saturday.

I have tried to dismount the fears of those ultra-Orthodox dykes who think that the nuns support Hitler or are in collusion with the Palestine Liberation Organization; so far, nothing has worked. To date, I have seen zero ultra-Orthodox Jewish or Zionist lesbians studying there. Also, my more religious peeps have shown little confidence to negotiate with this school because apparently, and I've heard this from some reliable sources, there is an arts and crafts class where kids make blue-and-white chastity belts.

Sister Jewniversity has always been problematic for Sapphic Orthodox Jews who live near it. To begin with, the black-coated scholars are not fond of the university moniker, "Sister Jewniversity," and have asked the Congressional Appropriations Education Committee to defund the school until it switches to a less anti-Semitic name.

The Hebe lezzies have prayed, argued and prayed, and when they were done, they issued this statement: "Woody Allen and Philip Roth employ self-derision in their diatribes, but *they are our diatribes*. Sister Jewniversity belongs to the same group that burned us during the Inquisition."

These Yiddish vigilantes, during their intense surveillance of Sister Jewniversity, observed my ex Emily eating scrambled eggs in a kosher diner known for its political discourse. She was wearing a habit, all black, and an earring in her nose. It was not clear if Emily was contemplating her Yiddish-lesbian roots or the possibility of being married to Christ for the rest of her life. Others considered Emily's inevitable Catholic conversion a reaction to her father being overly Jewish when he was younger, but *not allowing Emily to hang out with the ultra-Orthodox Sapphos in her neighborhood.* "Resentments," she once told me, "have a strange way of manifesting."

To remain close to her people, but to not alienate herself from the Catholic institution that provided her with an income, Emily went vegan and ate at IHOP. Some expected that she would go "Muslim" on us, as her puritanical garb was also comparable to what the Sunnis wore.

Emily, upon becoming a "nun," resented "imperial Zionists," particularly the Orthodox Jewish lesbians who opened kosher coffee houses in the West Bank.

* * *

Several members of the Orthodox Jewish Lesbian Espionage Society (OJLES) suspected that Emily held an unabashed allegiance to Ayn Rand, who was considered, quite possibly, one of Emily's personalities. For example, when Ayn Rand crosses the street, she does so without a cane, because she, Ayn Rand, does not want to be symbolically dependent on anything but her own invulnerability. This is also true with Emily, who has fallen numerous times, due to the influence of Ayn Rand and a lack of cane and/or prosthetic support system.

This may be why, after all the years Emily spent pursuing a Jewish education without her father's approval, it was time to become Catholic. She married a Catholic, but this made her less anti-Semitic and more Jewish because the Catholic that she married was a dirt bomb and his mother was even dirtier (this led Emily to remain part-time Jewish before she entered the convent).

* * *

Emily's characters to date: Jewish/nun/assistant endocrinologist; Jesuit fighter on behalf of the PLO; anti-Catholic dirt bomb activist; and Ayn Rand's protégé.

* * *

Emily thought, because she was gay in addition to being homophobic, "At least nuns don't have to worry about being lesbians. They just are what they are." This was pre-Pope, the new pope who kinda likes the gays and yet may have been involved in some underhanded minutiae with the Argentine militia in the eighties.

* * *

Unlike the Pope, Emily, in the eighties, had many personalities: she was a purveyor of Salisbury steaks; a punk rocker; a bike rider; and a habitual reader of illustrated French existential works.

Most people in Emily's high school, who disputed her being "schizoid," were transfixed by her gorgeousness and brilliance. She was too sultry, dreamy and inescapably attractive to be considered irrational.

Indeed, I still have dreams where Emily takes me aside and says, "You're looking good again." *I melt.* Just when you think this chick is a nutcase whom Sappho should burn at the stake, you are mesmerized by her soulful words.

* * *

That Emily had been my girlfriend, but then transformed into a nun, infuriated the Orthodox lesbians who felt that if I had at least separated my milk from meat—*set a good example*—I could have brought her into the fold.

* * *

Too much sex, even bad sex, is not good for anyone's soul. Of course, being that Emily was plump with skinniness, resembled the best tree in the orchard, the *sistahs* permitted her to enter with the preconditioned solicitation, "That I have never been, nor will I ever be, a lesbian or an anti-Semite, but it's alright if my political views diverge from the State of Israel and Orthodox-Zionist lesbians but still maintain sympathies with the PLO." Hamas was quiet back then, so most people considered Arafat and his boys the underdogs of the eighties.

* * *

When I convinced Emily to have sex with me, she declared that my dissimilar voices, which hollered at multifarious levels, inhibited her orgasm.

"It was impossible to distinguish the moans from the groans," she testified in front of the Sister Jewniversity Ethics Committee, adding, "Agatha Ravine's DIDD (dissociative identity disorder database) inspired me to take a vow and terminate all ties with cunnilingus."

Though Emily, I believed, had umpteen individualities (she reenacted the virtues and vices of Civil War nurses from the Confederacy or was a boy scout in 1968 in Illinois who had gone fishing), the Church gave her a nun permit. Emily was also paid a generous stipend to give lectures about how I was the malevolent "Judette" who was not kind to Palestinians.

Though I'm *not an Orthodox kike dyke who drives poorly on all days but the Sabbath*, I was considered far more sinister. I was "evilness minus the yeshiva."

"Stay away from Agatha Ravine. *You can't tell from one day to the next who she will be!*" Emily and her fellow nuns shouted when I dined at IHOP.

"*Agatha Ravine*," the enigmatic way she says, "Agatha Ravine," lyricism flies off the vowels. There were many nun-girls, some pretty, some with a few acne moments, who posted signs on the concrete lawn near IHOP, "Agatha Ravine is comprised of numerous characters. Please beware." My Muslim neighbors, dining on eggs with cheese, were confused because they considered me "the harmless Jew girl in the neighborhood who occasionally taxes us mentally."

* * *

Emily was very committed to her newfound role as postulant. And though the sisters knew she was Jewish with mixed philosophies like a beagle mutt, they printed a decree that read, "Be it known, that Emily, of Lizaville, New Jersey, may reside, in spirit, at Sister Jewniversity, as a nun, though her original intention was to become an endocrinologist's assistant. We like the presence of steamy women who maintain a hermetic presence that causes hormone overflow. Plus, Emily has been the victim of our enemy, Agatha Ravine, and we must all bond to make the world free of infidels."

On behalf of Sister Jewniversity, Emily would also be the anti-ultra-Orthodox lesbian character assassinator.

The Orthodox, realizing their nemesis was my nemesis, asked me to join their team and decry Emily's alluring sex appeal. I told them, rather straightforwardly, "It can never be argued that Emily has a non-good body. It is among the best, curviest and small and accessible from all angles. Her breasts are not the *boobiest,* but we don't necessarily blame her for this, particularly if her whiny voice during orgasm sounds like a combination of Gumby and Nina Simone."

Originally, Emily and I knew, based on our reputations, who we were. We also had a mutual friend, Dope, who had a five-minute relationship with Emily, when Emily put her hands around Dope's large boobs near the bathroom faucet. It was a stretch, for Emily has not always been able to grope boobs, but since hers were miniscule in comparison to Dope's, she was able to do more than just an erotic bear hug, and so romantically/unexpectedly, that Dope, who was known to dine on peanut butter and corn flakes at Zionist camp, nearly fainted.

[Midpoint digression: After Emily and I bumped into one another in the latrine at Sister Jewniversity, and I returned from my trip to Connecticut where the WASP had failed to exist and/or provide better resources on the Renaissance than Sister Jewniversity's library, Dope made us a lovely brunch of cornflakes and peanut butter and Emily and I became lovers.]

Emily and I encountered one another on that puerile level of skin where, if you rub one another too hard, you might get impetigo, like you did as a kid in the sandbox. Yes, we were always jumping on one another as if we had been without each other all our lives, which we had. And I thought: why should sex be the reason for your existence? Why can't we play Scrabble and she'll beat me, but it will create a more enduring relationship than this bestial relationship we have under the covers?

These multiple questions and concerns were too complex for Emily to comprehend so she blamed me for our failed relationship.

Emily declared, "Don't talk with Agatha! She has more characters than a William Faulkner novel."

To support her theories about me being the one with the misguided people in my cerebrum, she recalled a conversation I had told her about an ex who did, in fact, suffer from a personality disorder.

"I had a girlfriend who didn't know who she was. She brushed her teeth as a Wall Street janitor, and then flossed as a hippie," I told Emily.

My having this ex-girlfriend led Emily to believe I had caught this personality disorder as a sexually transmitted disease. She had me checked for this mental illness, in addition to AIDS, gonorrhea and a yeast infection, which she accused me of giving her.

"I feel like Wonder Bread!" she said the first time she came.

"Well, Emily, there are many organisms who'd like to interfere with our fun times, and I doubt it's personal."

Emily insisted that I take green pills before we sleep together.

"This will prevent more than one character from yelling out at once!"

As we became lovers, and she lost interest in her assistant endocrinology studies, Emily began to avoid me.

I didn't hear from her until we had lunch at Red Lobster.

"You are like my father, my mother, my brother, my dead aunts," she said, "they all speak through you. I am going to rename you Ouija Board—pre- and post-modern."

"I like your father," I said, because his pretentiousness was almost as charming as mine.

"*I'm not going to have sex with my father.* I was up all night all eating Hershey bars thinking *you were him.* This is appalling. It undermines my ability to stay thin and now that I'm considering the convent life—*well*—*I'm not in love with you 'cause I don't know who* 'you' *are...*"

And over peanuts, in this suburban restaurant where the beer floats high on the mugs, the mugs having been in the freezer, Emily left me unattended, unattached and without remorse.

THIS GIRL MARIA

MARIA HAS A CRUSH ON me.

She is half Renaissance Italian and half Reformation Greek.

Her father is a fireman.

She wears lipstick on top of a large body; she has the grace of a ballerina.

This should appeal to me, but I really don't want to go downtown on her.

I like girls who are androgynous or WASP-y and she fits neither category.

* * *

I traveled to Jamaicatown with her for the weekend because I assumed we would slowly evolve into a relationship. The optimal word is slow.

I quoted Molly Bloom because yes, I'd finally say yes to a relationship, except that yes to a relationship didn't mean yes to Maria.

Yes, after my Orthodox Jewish psychologist Mitchell had been an absolute prick and completely unavailable (i.e., falls asleep during the session), I pondered the short-time possibility of Maria. She was the psychological rebound. Usually when Mitchell's a prick I scan the Aetna Health Insurance website for a new shrink; this time I thought the best form of revenge would be to meet a someone.

* *· *

Maria had just purchased a huge house in Brooklyn. It was seventies Victorian, and although my dog peed on her bedspread, she wanted me to move in.

"I'm the perfect person to get impregnated with," she said. We'd use her brother's sperm and have blue-collar, intellectual babies.

* * *

While driving to "J-town," which is what dykes and fags call "Jamaicatown," she asked if I ever read *Stone Butch Blues*. She, like other box lickers who lust for me, assumes that I am a butch.

I wear homeboy hats and male clothes, but do so out of habit, having brothers and not sisters. I am a boy's boy, not a lesbian's butch. There is a difference: I hang out with gay boys at twelve-step meetings. Does this mean I'm a butch or a bitch?

I would never wear a three-piece suit.

I cut my hair short.

If anything, I would get a sex change operation to become a gay man.

I used to be the aggressor in male-to-male relationships on phone sex lines. They liked my voice, which was boyish. I liked fem guys. But after years of therapy, this ended and I couldn't fuck them over the phone. Besides, eventually they want to meet you and I don't have a scrotum.

* * *

Maria, a femme's femme, believes women will treat her better than guys. Dykes, however, also want skinny *shiksas*.

I gaze around my office and observe that the men date big ladies and consider Maria *a whalelike woman*.

I didn't like her when she walked up to my apartment. She wore hideous makeup—a blowfish with Maybelline concealing her fins. I am worried that God will punish me for not liking thickset women who are inherently amphibious.

Perhaps I will become a chubby girl again. The Atkins diet has stopped working. I just drank a Frappuccino and ate a delicious bun.

I have a membership to the New York Health and Racquet Club, except there is an annoying cleaning lady in the locker room who repeatedly says, "You don't fit into your clothes."

* * *

Maria drove me to J-town and said that we could ask each other questions, whatever came to us.

"I have a crush on you, do you like me?"

"Of course," I told her. "I wouldn't be here if I didn't feel that way."

You must understand: people who want you will hang onto your every word because they can make hours out of seconds. They interpret your statements with more zeal than Joycean scholars who analyze the author's fingerprints on toilet paper.

Maria, the Greek/Italian, wanted to bed me. I didn't want to bed her. So, the vinegar not mixing with oil began to muster.

When we arrived at our J-town rental (three hours later than most people because Maria was paying attention to me and not the speed of her car), we chose rooms.

Initially, she wanted the suite with the minimalist polyester design. I asked for the same room. She said I could have it (with chair and TV) if I let her watch *The Daily Show*. Although this was obviously manipulative on her part, I conceded, and said that I would surely permit her to use my space if she watched only TV.

* * *

That evening, after lobster and dancing, we got into night garbs. I wore an Eeyore nightgown; it was on sale, post-Xmas.

She wore a shirt.

Her large cellulite particles unmasked themselves.

As I've said, rotund women think that because I am tall and have short hair and a deep voice that I am their hoydenish fantasy come true. They forget that I am attracted to young/angular beings. I am not unlike Philip Roth in this regard.

* * *

A supposed friend, Martha, orchestrated this Maria nightmare. I told her that I was not into Maria.

Martha, who is a renowned poontang expert, advised me years ago, "You either dig a woman or you don't." If you don't feel like using that Latin word on the lower female organs, you shouldn't.

* * *

Maria had this ability to get me to agree to almost everything.

She got on my bed.

She looked into my eyes.

Maria has black hair and spends many hours arranging it.

She blow-dries to compensate for the fact that she is not anorexic.

She moves closer and says, "I like your eyes and your mind."

"I don't want to sleep with you," I say.

She remains quiet.

"I'm not ready to sleep with you," I whisper.

I hear her breathing inches away.

"What then?" I try not to renege on my refusal.

"I want to hold you."

She wanted to hold me after we had eaten lobsters and danced. The other ladies thought we were a couple. They reached a state of jubilance when we left the bar.

"I'm not attracted to you."

"What do you mean?"

"My therapist wants me to be honest with people. Don't fixate on me."

She left.

Then, thereafter, there were many notes and stares until we departed.

We were right for each other.

We were both emotionally distraught people.

I should sleep with her.

Give her a chance.

Stop being religious about the ones who are not really icons.

* * *

Stop my quest, quite frankly, for the perfect Wellesley sister and *shtup* Maria wildly and live in Brooklyn impregnated with her brother's blue-collar genes and send our kids to Catholic schools.

She's perfect for me.

A social worker, she is.

"You don't like being *too familiar*," was one thing she said.

"I think we're like sisters," I said.

"I don't think so."

Since we are so alike, she feels we must be soul mates and live our lives together.

* * *

Four love notes were sent, each the length of this story. They hinted, as love notes will, that we should meld.

Maria, who could have been an obese *faygelah*[5] with a bird named Bubka with compelling, sweet eyes, was completely devoted to me as spouse.

She would have helped me paint my apartment and sand my floors.

She'd teach me to drive.

---

5 Derogatory Yiddish term for "gay man."

I believe that by my writing this, her grandmother, who died two years ago, is going to kill me. *Or maybe her mother, who died just recently.*

I have that problem with women. Their dead relatives often want to murder me. On the way back from J-town we stopped off at an obscure Connecticut McDonald's where people dress in pearls and boat shoes, and the cashier said, "You're scum."

I was sure that an ex-obsession's dead father was after me, for why would the girl behind the McDonald's cash register call me "scum"? After all, my ex-infatuation had lived in this New England town, so I whispered numerous Hebrew prayers in the chain restaurant's bathroom.

* * *

My father is dead and so is my grandmother, which means I have two people who are ghosts/cherubs looking out for me. Besides, my grandmother recently had an affair with Eleanor Roosevelt.

* * *

I never cease to worry that my MacBook will be stolen or blow up as I compose this tale in Starbucks. The spirits from Heaven are quite excellent at destroying things.

But I, too, have powerful friends in Heaven who whisper in God's ears.

* * *

My therapist accuses me of not wanting intimacy.

"You should just roll over and get comfortable," he says, with a yarmulke dangling.

"Why act angry?" Martha says, holding her young Meryl Streep girlfriend.

Well, my answer to these people is, quite frankly, you can sleep with Maria if you want to.

I'd rather sleep with the Louise Browns[6] of the planet, or at least let them plant kisses, huge wet kisses, on my cheek. This is certainly more scintillating than a hug from Maria that would invariably crush me.

---

6   Louise Brown, born in 1978, was the first test tube baby. She is chubby and married to a nightclub doorman and has blonde hair and blue eyes.

KISSING A TREE SURGEON

I ONCE KISSED A TREE SURGEON from Lake Placid during a one-night tryst, so it was not considered such a big deal, though my friend Julie, who was ostensibly straight, kept coming into the bedroom while we were making out. She'd look in and close the door and stare over the covers where we snuggled and kissed. Apparently, I was permitted to have sex, but it wasn't clear if permissible meant acceptable to Julie.

I have always loved Julie, even today, though she is married and no longer speaks with me because I made anti-Julie's-boyfriend presents and gave them to her, in front of him. One year I gave her a crystal vase that said, "I love Prince Valium," and as her lover's last name was Valliantez, this was considered a faux pas. Most of the people at her birthday parties were surprised that Julie would invite me back each year, and I'd have yet another crystal vase with an unsavory message for him.

He was not without his unsavory messages for me. One year, after they were married, I called to speak with Julie, and since he knew my voice, he didn't bother to say hello and shouted, "Are you the only one on Earth *not watching the Super Bowl?*" he hung up.

Since that day of the Super Bowl hang up, she and I have not spoken.

The real cessation occurred, however, when Julie didn't invite me to her wedding.

I had been to her house, her favorite restaurant, had called her mother and stepfather to discuss my personal issues. I had bonded

113

with her brother who was an alcoholic. He condescendingly called me a "teetotaler."

Julie and I had even shared our deepest secrets while an Ethiopian cab driver, who had gotten his PhD in economics, hit his brakes with each new revelation he heard us discuss—his English was very good.

* * *

I was curious as to why I hadn't received an invite.

"Is there a reason you're not inviting me to your wedding?" I asked her.

"Yes, I'm not sure how you'd behave."

"I'm really hurt, I mean, I thought we were close, had a meaningful relationship."

"Sadism," she said, "particularly from your end, is not what I'd deem meaningful." Click. The click from a landline phone has always been distressing.

* * *

We hadn't spoken since they moved to Maine, where her husband was a communications professor specializing in Fox News. His thesis was that Gerald Ford's contribution to America was negligible compared with Richard M. Nixon's, though Nixon was still, as he is today, maligned in academic circles.

That she didn't invite me, I was so mortified, so astonished; I was the fairy godmother in *Sleeping Beauty* who is not invited to the wedding. Unlike the overlooked fairy godmother, however, I wouldn't, based on ethics derived from Martin Heidegger, ever cause a person to nap so long—they wouldn't know when their being had ended or begun because the sleep would induce mass levels of confusion.

* * *

But alas, it might have been the tree surgeon incident, more than the crystal vase writings or my other behavioral improprieties, including applying for a job at her office while she was still working there, that infuriated her.

* * *

Julie is drunk, and speechless, when she sees me making out with her old boyfriend Andrew's best friend—a tree surgeon who lives in Rye, New York. We are at Andrew's party where beer is on tap and hormones whir like gnats.

Julie had broken Andrew's heart because he was not Bohemian enough and did not grasp the meaning of her sonnets, though he had the right chromosomal lines to combine with hers.

Previously, Julie had assumed I was 100% lesbian and banned me from her bed, which was why I was startled by her behavior.

Julie *didn't like me that way*, and insisted I remain on the couch when I slept over, as if sleeping in her bed would do anything but obliterate my peace because she snored so loudly. She was absolutely convinced I might rape or seduce her or whatever expletives homophobic straight women on trust funds attending grad school in New York City uttered in the late eighties. Also, Julie had hosted Eudora Welty in her Manhattan apartment, and it would be sacrilegious, in her mind, to have an orgasm with me in the same space where Ms. Welty had made jokes about Southern bread and dispossessed janitors.

* * *

"What are you doing, Agatha?"

I am kissing the tree surgeon, whose blonde sultriness is overwhelming her.

"Agatha!"

Kissing is extremely difficult to stop, particularly when the beer has driven your mind to scintillating levels.

"Julie, do you mind?"

"Mind what?"

"I am trying to make out with what's his name," I say, hoping she will find no subtle reasons to remain in the room.

But she remains, just as she rages when I speak with other men or women who take time away from her. Julie is also not keen on our friend Alessandro who makes jokes that lead me to insatiable fits of laughter. She stares with impatience when I am oblivious to her.

Julie sits on the chair next to us; she, too, has had a few too many beers.

"Do you mind?" the tree surgeon asks.

"What?" she says, as if, in her drunken euphoria, there are ceiling tiles falling.

"We'd like some privacy," he says—my thoughts championing his. The tree surgeon is confused that I have a chaperone. It would be okay if Julie were joining, but no, she is levitating toward us.

"You guys have already shared this honeymoon—and we have school in the morning…"

"We…?"

"Ahhhh—c'mon Agatha, it's twelve a.m. and I must be going…"

"Julie—it's two a.m…and…"

"Well, if we don't go now, we won't get a ride home."

Julie gets my coat and throws it on top of us.

The tree surgeon releases me from his caress, and the mood is gone, like a wild oak that has been knocked over by the wind.

SHE GAVE ME A LIBERAL DOSE
OR
WHEN W INVADED IRAQ

I BECAME A LIBERAL WHEN I met her.

She was sitting in the audience at the Tribeca Film Festival and I said to myself, "She looks gay but I think she's straight," and when we finally met after opening night, her seat next to mine, I transformed from neoconservative to a liberal on the war in Iraq because endorsing Dick Cheney was not going to get me to the grand summit of lesbian orgasm. Plus, I think it's okay to temporarily exit my small world of predictable Republican gatherings, which include bitter Soviet immigrants with wool socks who attend libertarian meetings and drink iced tea. In addition, these ex-Soviets go to the beach with umbrellas and/or hit on me at frat parties. I'm usually not interested.

Of course, my true thoughts are: we should let the world sink or swim, but as Saddam Hussein slaughtered numerous Kurds, it is imperative that we bomb the shit out of him. This thinking, however, leaves little hope that you will get laid because lesbians with short hair at film festivals do not want to comprehend that you are particularly in love with them or the war. They like distance, heartache, a little game playing, some internet exploration, and a few words about why you were not at last week's peace rally or Whole Foods during the mad rush at Meatless Mondays between 5–7 p.m.

The female at the film festival is a lawyer. She works at a prestigious law firm and eats salad from Starbucks with a not-so-inexpensive vinaigrette. She's Starbucks socioeconomics. Between Tribeca Film Festival and walks through the Berkshires, she marches with Jersey girlfriends to protest "Bush" in the White House. But she does so with a sense of humor, a smirk, and a blink during the film's urine scenes where we are perplexed. We are perplexed because I am sitting with my mother, who is on the left and *she* is on my right, and how do I explain anonymous gay male sex in the Indonesian film to my mother, and that's why *she* blinks at me. The blinking, which is done so well—exquisite twenty-year-old eyelids—is no indication that we're going to...*you know.* I can't even get the energy to bump into her knee while she's chewing a brownie.

"Do you like that scene?"

"It's *brill.*" I say.

"Brill?"

"You know, brilliant."

She hopes that I will comment negatively about Nicole Kidman's repetitive performance in the Lars von Trier movie.

She also pesters me about the upcoming LGBTQ march in Washington next Tuesday. This chick is a rare breed of contemptuous progressive who sees movies and attends rallies and detests drama, which I find strange because war rallies comprise the neuroses of pragmatists who don't act out emotionally until they're yelling how much they abhor Cheney or his rightwing daughter (not the lesbian, though his lesbian *is conservative,* but not as vehement, I believe, as her hetero sister).

"Well," I say, remembering that my subscription to *National Review* will run out next week, "I'm not sure I can make it, but my support is unconditional."

She seems disappointed. There are dykes in New York City who don't understand when you say that you are a Republican. They envision Log Cabin Republican fags living in new condominium complexes in the West Village or Chelsea—indeed gay men can meander in that realm; but if you're female and not a fan of Kate Millett—don't believe Kate is the female Socrates of a new generation and the older ones for that matter—then you are behind the times, not the *New York Times*, the *Sappho Times*.

For years the pink triangle ladies have lambasted me. They consider me so self-involved that I am missing a link in an ideology that is about me. One former girlfriend left a message, "Why don't you try Buddhism instead of solipsism?"

This lawyer dates former biological men with insecurity complexes who are now present-tense women. She is that ripening between male and female. I might as well retire from dating because I don't fit into her exponential zone of hormones. They just keep popping all over the page like last year's fireworks and here I am an antiquated cherry bomb, hoping she'll celebrate with me. She dates post and pre-gender; she likes men-to-women or women-to-men who have become complex yet impassioned folks. It's all very discombobulating—a *Blade Runner* scenario where transgender humans, rather than replicants, replace cisgender males and females.

She's so discerning in her diminutive haircut and pleasing neck and luscious demeanor but giggles during the film's perspicuous moments.

She's David Carradine chasing Uma Thurman, she being the chaser of poor George Bush, Jr., a great man who merely wants to capture terrorists and fry them. I find nothing so exhilarating as that. Tell that to the queer thought police. Unless you are becoming a male-to-female version of Theodore Roosevelt (he had liberal leanings, though he did hunt elephants) you better forget quickwitted girls whose teeth resemble a Broadway theater curtain.

Lawyer girl is a riddle in God's path who enjoys my stories, smirks implicitly, likes my matter-of-fact idiosyncrasies, my tranquil persona. Doesn't dig my cellulite. What can we do to seduce twenty-year-olds weighing 120 pounds with a sweet temperament? We are two sad ships eclipsing generations. Plus, she's dating twenty people at once and trying to find herself though she's earnestly mature for her age.

Several of my friends who don't support her anti-war gatherings and could give two shits about the pro-PLO contingency she marches with—they'd rather be watching the war between the Yankees and Red Sox—say she likes me.

She gives me the same amount of attention during this film festival as my friend Rosamunde, who also sits with us. We all giggle at *Hell in Bangladesh*, a film in which when people sneeze you hear the footsteps in the background. Although it is based on Chekhov's *The Cherry Orchard*, they write "Inspired by Chekhov's *Cheery Orchard.*" The movie's melodrama is the antithesis of cheery. A young boy is eaten by a snake in the lake. We expect hell, the existence thereof, to be a place where one *is eaten* by a crocodile; the snake in the lake, which serves as the Freudian Bangladeshi basis for the tragedy, is not what we had in mind.

"Edward Said wrote that movies are a manifestation of Western imperialism," the attorney tells us.

"Isn't he dead? Didn't Professor Said pass away last Tuesday?"

"Did he? I didn't know that."

She wears bright red lipstick and black stockings and black shoes and resembles a totem pole.

We go to the local Starbucks, of course, because we both have Starbucks cards. This all goes according to my expensive cognitive therapist's advice, "Ask her out for coffee." If she says yes or no it will nevertheless determine my fate, like sticking my feet in water; is it cold or hot, should I dip in?

Pragmatists are not romantics. I still have not invited her to coffee. Therefore, she could not reject me.

However, today I asked her, in self-indulgent real time, "Will you be my lawyer?"

It did not work.

"Let's be friends." Whenever anyone uses the F word they don't likely mean the more vulgar F word.

When she refused to be my lawyer and instead chose to be my friend, I asked the people in my office, "If she wants to be my friend, does that mean she doesn't want to be my lawyer or that she doesn't want me to put my hand on her knee during the next screening?"

"Clearly," says Hank K, notorious for his confidence in his own viewpoints, "she wants to be your pal."

To get yet another opinion, I asked Sandra Piquet who lives in the Bronx and has an itinerant brainpower for reducing all of us to mere consonants while she stretches along the ocean as a vowel— loud and in-sync with the water's rhythms. An empty consonant has no destiny but to follow the vowel.

"You gotta be friends before you can be *enemas, I mean enemies.* Enemies are sexy, but friendships evolve to fights so don't wooooooooooooorry, you'll be fine."

I have changed my outer appearance, given into my nonrealistic political view, and made a tentative promise to go to a peace rally, where several pro-PLO groups will marvel at my "I am a Zionist" button.

"Will you come with me to the peace rally?" she asks.

"Is that all this will come to?"

"I think you can surmise this will not be sexual."

"You mean like two feather pillows shaking hands?"

"Like two doves rubbing beaks."

With that I decide to renew my subscription to the *National Review* and think about getting one to the *American Spectator.* George Bush, Jr., has been soliciting money for his second term and I place the fundraising campaign envelope conspicuously on my night table.

True, the embittered Soviet girls with woolen socks at the Young Republican meetings couldn't light a fire to my prima donna, but at least I won't have mindless conversations with blonde-haired Whole Foods cashiers to determine if my ATM card is working.

In the end, I go hear Mr. Norman Mailer speak at the Ninety-Second Street Y and decide that it's okay to see people like Norman as the multifaceted creatures they are: half liberal, half reactionary, with an extra plus—he makes fun of Robert Lowell, a quasi-liberal with a trust fund.

BOB AND PATTI

I NORMALLY DATE MYSELF, THOUGH THIS dude was a coffee cup away from me.

We were drinking and he pondered, "Are we in a relationship?"

When anyone aspires to remove me from my preamble, that is, an existence without another existence, I suffer their words and quietly refrain.

* * *

I like the space that exists in fire and air and all that occurs when burning is the sensation.

* * *

He had an earring in his nose and a moustache that swooped me.

I could not talk when he gazed and described his latest, greatest and favorite Bob Dylan album.

I am not a Bob Dylan fan, nor do I like Patti Smith, but he wanted me to attend their concerts.

* * *

As you know, this is no way to keep love brewing when your thoughts are like a paragraph from Margaret Atwood's *The Handmaid's Tale*.

Still, I agreed to sleep there for a night.

Just a night.

* * *

He kept gawking.

In the pink room, where many people remove their despair, he followed my eyes, which led to the coffee shop.

"Do you mind if I sit down?"

He took my hand.

We discussed hip-hop and The Mekons and The Ramones. For him it is and always will be about music and the great void it leaves in his soul.

It is music that is the wildest conundrum.

* * *

He has never forgiven me for my disparaging remarks about Dylan and Ms. Smith.

"You need to be more respectful," he whispered.

I declined more bourbon that evening.

I fell in a state of calm and did exercises learned at the psychiatrist's. This included sticking my stomach out and breathing in and out.

He could not fathom the bourbon wasted. He drank my cup.

We went to the fire and held hands, but his eclipsed mine rather than held it.

He clung to metaphors from songs.

The alcohol was firing, his grandmother was dead, and Patti and Bob made all things right.

LAVINA

"D O YOU DRIVE A CAR?" she asked on the way to Hyannis.
"No."
"Is it because you have a handicap?"
I had never passed my written test.

I also felt as estranged from driving a car as I did taking Stanley Kaplan's GRE prep course.

* * *

Lavina, while driving, explained where Hyannis was. She was perplexed by my inability to grasp the logic of her map.

"Did you also fail geography?" she asked. "Maybe you have a directional disability? Anyway, what do you do for a living?"

"I work at a prophylactics factory in the Bronx," I said.

"Don't you want to do something more important?"

Lavina lived in a duplex apartment in Brooklyn and owned a house in Hyannis.

"No, I'm happy," I lied.

There was no point in currying favor or disfavor. Let her win the argument. There are no room/board charges if she wins the argument. If she loses and you win, then you lose because invariably you will pay.

"Yes, you're right, perhaps the rubber business is not very prestigious."

"Maybe you should try hosiery?"

"Sure."

"They give you pensions in the hosiery business. You don't get that with condoms. Besides, what's a nice Jewish girl like you working with rubbers?"

It's true. My friends were lobbyists for gun companies or copy editors for clients who made butter. It was a small world, and they all knew each other, and gave each other jobs, though not me.

"I have some friends in the hosiery business. Did you go to college?" she asked.

"Yes."

"Where?"

"Staten Island State."

"Is that why you're working with rubbers?"

"No, my father said it would help diminish my anger toward men."

"What does that mean?"

"He said that if I could appreciate that their lives depend on a small piece of synthetic material, I could understand their vulnerability."

"You're not a lesbian, are you?"

"No."

"Good, I don't like lesbians. I think my ex daughter-in-law is one." Lavina turned red like her Subaru.

* * *

Lavina was rather insistent, in general. She was particularly insistent that her neighbor, a "New Age dyke who is a smart businesswoman," was responsible for the backward spiral of Lavina's once sanctimonious rule over a people-free neighborhood on their Hyannis street.

The woman had a Jack Russell who barked nonstop.

"Shut the fuck up!" Lavina yelled at the wooden house where the canine lived. The house had been built by a gluten-free construction company and you could hear everything outside.

She was annoyed at this "dumb *shiksa*" for a multitude of

reasons, and most recently, because the woman was "opening another store in Hyannis."

It was unclear where Lavina's antipathy toward lesbians and their money originated.

Lavina's former daughter-in-law, whom she accused of being a "radical gay," said Lavina "molested" her kid.

"All I did was spank the girl. These politically correct types," she said, "are worse than Stalinists." Lavina had family members murdered by Stalin, which gave her a bitter view of anything that "veered near communist ideology."

As for "molesting her granddaughter," Lavina was more a disciple of brain molestation. She could take your brain and make you feel as if she were your resident lobotomist.

Her "brain molestation" techniques were also in her art—abstract blue-and-green smegma patterns—she captured the essence of smegma in batik.

A critic in *ARTnews* had written, "Lavina Schwartz is more on top of this subject matter than Philip Roth."

"That's what we have in common," I mentioned to Lavina, "I work with rubbers, and you concern yourself with what goes inside of them."

"You know *nothing* about my work!" she said. "You know zero about the theoretical precedence of smegma and its expression through batik."

"But I work with rubbers," I added.

"You're just a blue-collar factory worker."

There were a few moments of silence.

"I'm sorry," she glanced at me, "did I offend you?"

It's very characteristic of me not to defend myself. I lapse into passive/aggressive inarticulateness, which causes the said person who has caused me neurological pain to suffer.

"No," I said, "I'm just in the middle of a Philip Roth book and I'd like to finish it."

"Oh—which one is that?"

"*The Breast*."

"Is that where the main character gets breast cancer?"

"No, it's about a man who turns into a breast."

"Oh…" Her "oohs" were self-effacing. You knew, and she knew, the argument, like a tedious chess game, had not gone in her favor.

"Have you gotten your bus schedule for tomorrow?" she asked me. "I won't be able to drive you."

"Yes."

"Good."

"Remember," I said to myself, as I took *The Breast* to bed, "nothing in this world is free, and when it is, it is insufferable."

HORSE CARRIAGE
AND BED BUGS

"I'M THE MAN NOW," HER husband told me at Marie's wedding. During the first few minutes I met him, an intellectual from Florence, Italy, who behaved like a kid, I realized they shouldn't have children.

Marie, on the other hand, ignited a room.

She loved the golden silk shirt I wore to their wedding.

"You look delightful," she said when he was not nearby.

* * *

Marie was only unfaithful to me in our poetry class at Columbia University where she sided with those who felt my words were slightly inferior to those of William Butler Yeats.

* * *

Marie was better than most humans: no judgment—just hugs and euphoric remarks when I said something funny or perceptive.

She was my editor, because my grammar was terrible, and she often made corrections.

A friend said she wanted me, no doubt. Everyone knew this, he said.

It's true; we held hands on the subway, long before the bed bugs arrived.

I figured we were lovers in an intrepid state where the winds passed and we masked our truer intentions.

* * *

Marie was my employer, on a part-time basis, and I told her, when she hired a former coworker, "You should not hire Sam Jann, the graphic designer."

He was hired the day before Tuesday, when Marie and her colleagues decided I should be let go.

* * *

It became a slippery slope when Marie informed my coworkers she'd banish me. They were eating curry chicken and Pentimento cheese sandwiches with vichyssoise.

Banish me from the workplace.

"You're going to hire Sam Jann?" I asked.

"Everyone loves him." He was tall, brown-haired and had dimples.

Sam, whose dimples I had known since pre-nursery school, was likable and more female than me.

He and his wife were my friends. I occasionally had coffee with them, though they were possessive and resented my visiting the Empire State Building and not them.

At work, just after one day, Sam's popularity escalated.

I traveled with Marie to the office comfort zones, telling her I meant well, but she kept crying. She didn't want to say goodbye, but it was like in poetry class, where the opinion was against me.

"You need to hire Sam Jann and fire me?"

"There's a new trend in industry," she said, which meant that everyone was cutting employees and expanding companies.

* * *

I said mean things about her throughout the office.

I pointed at her long nails and noted how unappealing they were—so unlike the Philadelphia suburb she grew up in.

She also had tyrannical mood swings that impeded small talk, particularly after she had endured a temper tantrum from her groom.

Probably the most disrespectful thing I said was, "Your breasts are flat." This did not sit well with people who reported to her in the lingerie department.

* * *

I thought I could preclude termination by advising Marie about her niece, who was now in "recovery."

It's good to have a conversation that you have not yet had and have it while you can or at least let it linger in the back of your mind so that others sense there are things you have not yet discussed but will be of importance to them when you do.

Marie's niece was a heroin addict whom I befriended before Marie married the Florentine who declared at his wedding, "I am the man."

We were in the final moments of my employment.

We were riding on a horse-driven carriage near Central Park, trying to avoid the subway bed bugs, which might have also been on the buses.

"There she is!" Marie said. It was her niece, the heroin addict, in heels and walking toward us.

This was disheartening because *I had* wanted to tell her about the young girl's recovery.

It was my last attempt to secure a position in the office; that we, the heroin addict and me, knew each other from meetings. We exemplified the lost kids—the girls who don't make it to the altar to say, "I do" or "I will"; the ones who are marked in poetry class

as "The non–New York Times Best Seller List"; the chicks who are
going to be passed over for the agreeable graphic designers/editors
wearing a suit and tie with mighty connections, which means they
can sit in their cubicles and read the great stock options they've
received from their new company.

"Are you sure you don't want to join us?" Marie asked.

I nodded.

My plot to renew her sympathies was foiled as she and her niece
went for lunch.

I was alone, on the street, while they rode in a brougham, the
horse treated to a carrot, and Marie, with sorrowful eyes, tears that
didn't abate, waved goodbye.

EMBRYONICS

AT OUR COMPANY, WE STEWED embryos, cooked them in a large egg yolk facility and turned them into receptor chords for life.

She employed me based on my resume because I didn't do well on the tests. Some people don't perform well on tests, she said.

But you'd fit in here, she said, and hired me.

I heard the place was very bohemian. They let you say or do *whatever*. The head honchos were facetious. It was okay to breathe, just keep the volume down.

There was a lunchroom and a soda machine and big bathrooms. The bathrooms weren't marked "ladies" or "men," so we sat in them for long minutes.

The woman who hired us, the best boss you could have, was always nervous. She wrote stories.

We got along fine until one day she said, "Look, I don't agree with you. Living in New York as an adolescent was just as hard as New Jersey."

I assumed people could remain unnoticed in Manhattan; whereas New Jersey was an undercrowded can of sardines where teens tortured children who did not care for Led Zeppelin.

She contended that New York City could also be a troublesome locale for adolescents. Maybe the homeless picked on her.

After that conversation, she didn't beam as much, although both of us were in "the program," but neither of us pretended to like each other.

The last time we spoke she said, "Diane Lewis, you're a very pleasant and intelligent person, but I'm going to have to let you go."

Let go. Gone. See ya.

She's such an agreeable person. How can such a likable individual fire a girl like me? They say it had to do with my inability to pick up things. I missed them. *You missed them.* But if people are in "the program," aren't they supposed to watch over you? Especially your supervisor—isn't she supposed to be a mentor not a *preventer*?

The Right to Life movement was funding us; but did this mean you couldn't miss a few eggs now and then or it's "See ya later?"

The eggs fell on the floor. My boss got upset.

"The graphic designer said you got yolk all over his computer!"

What I couldn't comprehend was why they placed the advertising department so close to the lab.

"We want to make sure the creative staff understands our clientele."

Eggs. That's what we did for a living. In our office it was called "the incubator grind."

"And if one green eggy should accidentally fall, there will be two green eggies standing on the wall."

I sang that with the other embryonics comrades as we struggled with microscopic equipment to ensure that the embryos were sanguine with the sperm we dropped in their test tubes.

Eggs are very particular about the sperm that fall in their test tubes. It's sort of like dating. If *you're not* into the disco hermaphrodite you met last Tuesday—he doesn't remind you of John Travolta—you're probably gonna commit suicide if the hermaphrodite enters.

Each test tube contains irascible sperm. Sometimes the sperm are kind, but you know most men—they're irascible. This is the reason so many test tube problems occur. Feminists think that they can live without men. *It's not true.* You need a sperm to form your reproductive utopia. And what do you think—you're just going to get yeshiva boys? No, Hasidim and feminists alike cannot predict whether their sons or daughters will wear tattoos or whether they will be punk rock nurses on the Haitian war front fighting against

Asian imperialists. We all have a difficult time in life predicting the future.

That's why I like George Clooney. He exudes sunniness. If the sperm, let's say, is a George Clooney–like seed, it makes me tremble.

If I'm an egg, right, and I'm going to let some sperm drop into my test tube, I look to see how the sperm sweats. If he sweats like a Republican, I let him dive in like a torpedo. If the sperm is an effeminate nose wipe who got his doctoral degree in analyzing watermelon rinds in the shape of anal tracks, then I say: *"Later babe, I ain't procreating with no brownnosing fop!"*

Anyway, returning to my sperm/egg/embryonics lab, I started getting into embarrassing situations because I'd say things such as, "What came first, the sperm or the egg?" while clients were visiting.

Freelance unconventional workers in embryonics labs have little raillery. Most hook up with infertile corporate vice presidents, for workplace eccentrics are truly corporate sluts.

I, too, am a corporate wannabe and buy Banana Republic shirts. Last Tuesday I wore a new purple one, hoping that an account exec would ask me to dinner.

I know, I want to be a bohemian and write about the plagues of my time, but I also enjoy moving up the corporate ladder. I like ladders. When I was five years old, I remember being on a fire truck in a parade.

But returning to this insecure boss: she writes fiction. Her name is unknown. We know her by the way she grunts. We just know her persona, her soul, her humor. We, at the Right to Life Embryonics Lab, are completely enamored with grunts—noises that indicate life is different inside a person.

When "Grunty," our boss, grunts, we can distinguish her from other grunters—her grunts are more insecure. It sounds like peanuts getting stuck in an elephant's trunk. Most grunters are not as indecisive with the grunts as she is; that's what makes her special.

But when she told me I was no longer going to work in the embryonics lab, I was devastated. *It was my obnoxiousness. It was my Banana Republic shirts. It was the sneakers I wore consecutively—forgetting the rubber shoes that make me fall off ladders.*

"No," she said, "you keep dropping eggs on the floor. How can you be an embryonics engineer if you continuously drop eggs on the floor? The Right to Life president thinks you've killed a few Pat Robertsons and William F. Buckley, Juniors. Even though you are pleasing and bright, I'm going to let you go."

I was stunned. I thought a colossal Cimmerian grove fell upon my head. I believed my grandmother had peed on me from Heaven. All my hopes and ambitions (i.e., my longing to visit France and eat Ben & Jerry's ice cream at the Eiffel Tower next summer on my embryonics paycheck) were thrown astray. No more on-sale shirts from Banana Republic. No more attempts to convince the account execs that I was a droll, quick-witted nonconformist from the East Village who could fascinate their corporate friends. I was told to bring in my time sheet and not play with eggs.

I still hear grunts on occasion and know it's not paramecium rioting in my interiors; rather, it's the nasal appendages of my former boss smelling to see if I'm still doing well in the world. Some people are not prepared for the complications of embryonics. Some of us are simple nine-to-five secretaries or shoelace saleswomen. That's okay. It's great for me to remember where it all began and that at one time, I had something to do with it.

THE GIRL WITHOUT
MAKEUP

WHEN ONE LOOKS AT A girl without makeup who normally covers her face, it is shocking, particularly before class begins.

Such was the case with Alexandra Q.

She was not an outstanding mind, though she did well in economics.

She met her husband at a frat where Jewish men either married the women they didn't sleep with or slept with the ones they didn't marry.

Alexandra Q was the type who gets married, stays married, and takes her economics major to untethered levels.

I was disturbed that Alexandra Q, a Jew bred on gefilte fish, was not even remotely accomplished like Jews from my high school. Indeed, she was an insatiable non-wunderkind with zero bounce in her feet, flat chested and not the least bit interested in poontang.

At least my grandmother, Ida, may she rest in peace, cut her toenails in bed while peeling carrots. Some may not consider this an enviable skill, that is, multitasking in bed, but Grandma was capable of entertaining kids and grandkids and accomplishing much in her bed whereas most people merely sleep in theirs.

Alexandra Q stayed home, made macaroni and cheese, put said macaroni and cheese in a Tupperware container, and took it to class, where she ate in the biology lab because she was disgusted by odors in the college cafeteria.

Alexandra Q is the girl you see on the stairs whose work is more prized than her relationships with people, and will brag to you, "Yes, I have housebroken my dog." She is a brilliant person who can housebreak a dog in five minutes whereas most of us face the dilemma of a few months before doggy stops committing those salacious acts.

Alexandra is, without exception, the serial mom portrayed by Kathleen Turner who is insistent that the poor fucking puppy not shit in house. Don't wear white after September, don't defecate on my wooden floors. And God forbid the shag rug you shit on dear puppy—that might land you in Hades.

* * *

Alexandra Q, thus it came to pass, moved in with her husband in the suburbs.

They did not lead an extraordinary life.

They didn't spend an enormous amount of money at Whole Foods.

She was still the girl who looked bad without makeup because she had worn makeup her entire life and would be like someone who stops eating donuts and no longer has a donut-like disposition or papier mâché face.

* * *

Alexandra Q lived with her husband in a mansion on Eighth Street that could have been a tree house or hiding space for the underground railroad during slavery times because there were many unopened compartments that weren't opened unless you knew they were there.

Her husband was a prosperous dermatologist who, when he needed to make more money, would tell kids and their moms that to really prepare their epidermal layers for next week's hurricane, they should get hormone injections; it would give their skin more resilience and prevent them from losing face in a storm that would devastate the coastline.

She was the rat for her husband's dermatology experiments, which caused even more protrusions in her face.

This might explain why, without makeup, his wife's face became multi-layered; whereas her brother, Simon, had a remarkably normal face that did not have the streams or currents that afflicted her.

Alexandra Q also provided the data that made his profits possible, though some parents had doubts.

"I'm still not certain why the hormone shots are necessary for the hurricanes," one mother said to the dermatologist.

"Well," he said, "when wind blows ferociously against your face, the skin requires a heaviness for protection. Hence, the use of hormones, which makes the skin heavier, will combat this problem."

"Are we expecting a hurricane?"

"Any day now," he said.

* * *

The beautiful girl's husband, who had seen me during their fraternity days—me, always in the corner, watching Alexandra Q breathe and steal fruit from the cocktail drinks in the fraternity—suspected I might have a crush on his wife. Thus, he had a security guard (and several members of the Elks Club, including an adolescent boy who removed the cherry from his daughter in a Corvette when she was fourteen) residing at his Eighth Street mansion.

Not on purpose, or perhaps on purpose, I frequently went by their house and spied to see if *she* was there. It was always on the way, no matter where I was going.

I did not pursue her because she was beautiful with makeup.

I simply wanted to sleep with her.

It's like Formica—you know it's a stupendous element in your kitchen and you want to kiss it—to touch and feel the cool, smooth ambiguous nature of it.

Finally, when the weather was freezing and the Hasidic Jews were not driving along Eighth Street—*they are bad drivers for the most part who think about God, not buses or pedestrians*—it was Shabbat—I walked near her house.

I was dressed in black.

I stared through the doors.

Unexpectedly I saw people gazing at me—the security guard and his Elks Club friends.

As I was in black, it was impossible for them to recognize who I was or could have been in a different lifetime.

It's not like I knew them, or they knew me, but they were clearly being paid by her husband the dermatologist to look for me.

However, I didn't resemble me, and was clearly someone else—someone not the least bit impertinent—and they thought: *Who is this? Doesn't look like "HER." Could it be her?*

I ran—that is, I took my feet, which were extended by my titanium knees and hip, and in the dark of night, where I was the only one resembling a Hasidic Jew—*along Eighth Street*. Everyone could see my butt, which is large, but the butt, in the black of night, was black, so they could only tell the dermatologist, in an accurate and truthful way, "We saw black on black. We're not 100% sure it was her."

* * *

Last night I invaded their house again.

This time it was in Little Italy, NY, where I owe the mafia a lot of money: eight hundred dollars, to be exact, which has garnered interest over the years.

If the mafia catches me, and I don't have this money, they will kill me.

Thus, knowing that the mafia would be reluctant to enter the dermatologist's apartment in Little Italy on Centre Market Place, right behind the old police building where Toni Morrison (with Rastafarian hairdo) lived—and I did wave to her once—thousands of people have likely waved to her—I came upon the dermatologist's New York apartment.

I had previously lived in his apartment, when it was *not worth five million dollars*. Now it is worth five million dollars, but despite my not living there—I could only afford eight hundred dollars a month—I had mail addressed to me that still came to that address, which the current residents threw on the floor. It piled up, sometimes dated, with dead relatives' handwriting appearing on unopened letters.

The new residents, who had furnished apartments with maligned paintings that would be repugnant to people who knew anything about art, were quite friendly.

There was only one indignant person present in the building last night, likely a good friend of the dermatologist and his wife, who was not enamored by my presence.

"What the hell are you doing here?" he asked in an Austrian accent. He had not seen me since we worked together in a bowling alley in Howell, New Jersey, and this seeing me, in such proximity, nearly caused him cardiac problems.

"I'm looking for that girl who is married to the dermatologist," I said, so the elderly Italian ladies, who were getting their mail, could hear me. They had been busy preparing pasta with ricotta cheese and homemade ravioli and there is no doubt that the gossip of my pursuing this woman, which was not looked upon well by the Austrian spy, added spice to their cooking sessions.

"But I used to live here," I said.

"Not anymore," the Austrian said.

"I'm still getting mail."

"Please leave at once or I'll call the police."

He, the Austrian, was the kind of perpetual narcissist who'd act like your friend when you were picking up pins together in the bowling alley, but once the job was over, he would certainly not invite you to hang out with him and his wife for a Coke at the bowling alley restaurant counter.

It was rumored he had a Jewish star painted in his toilet bowl, and whenever he peed, he giggled in a vicious and anti-Semitic manner. This "pee on Jewish star in toilet" appeared in several documentaries that have since been removed from Netflix because the dermatologist is on that company's board.

* * *

The Austrian kept a distance of several miles from me and other colleagues after work at the bowling alley because he believed that a worker was someone you could not avoid during working hours, and this meant you needn't socialize with them afterward.

* * *

The bowling alley job was reminiscent of the time I had been employed in a factory and was violent toward my colleagues. They nearly executed me and set me in concrete after the beating was over. There was a certain amount of redemption, but it was mostly that life was futile and I had to succumb to factory violence and a lack of superiority.

* * *

The Austrian had gone on to better things: he had become the dermatologist's spy.

He was hired while gossiping about me one day in the bowling alley restaurant.

"She is indefatigably the worst pin placer I've met. I've placed pins in Austria, Germany and now New Jersey. It's a mystery *why* they employ her."

The dermatologist, sitting next to the Austrian, quietly contemplated my stalking that led to his wife's reluctance to return damaged pantyhose to Macy's—knowing full well I'd get a new bra and watch her return merchandise—and was distressed by the current state of affairs.

"You know her?" he asked my fellow pin placer.

"Doesn't everyone?" he said in an Austrian accent with New Jersey nouns and adjectives.

"She's been hounding my wife since college. We are beyond ourselves. Clueless."

The Austrian was perplexed.

"What do you think I can do?"

"Prevent the stalking. Keep an eye on her. We have a place in New York where she has been getting her mail. Apparently, she used to live in our apartment *before* it was transformed from a rat-infested birthing spot to a multimillion-dollar condo. Just behind the old police building…"

"You mean the old police building where Richard Gere lived with Cindy Crawford?"

"Yes, and where Toni Morrison resided? Her Nobel Prize in Literature had skyrocketed the real estate prices. Ain't that amazing?"

"Not as amazing as her hair was," the Austrian said.

* * *

The juggernaut was that the Austrian confronted me while I was eating spaghetti in a Little Italy restaurant, which was infamous for smelling like pee.

"You need to stop bothering the girl," the Austrian said, while several felines climbed over my table.

"And what are you going to do about it?"

"We are going to lock you in a Manhattan solitary confinement cell," he said.

"What?"

"Waiter," he said to the man who was serving me pasta, "please remove this woman." The FBI had recently taken over this eating establishment so I was handcuffed and told that if I ever went near the girl with the beautiful face with makeup and/or her apartment or Eighth Street mansion, I would be locked in solitary confinement on Rikers Island. The FBI man gave me a bus ticket and I returned home.

* * *

Since then I have not seen the dermatologist, the Austrian or the girl with the beautiful face with makeup.

I've heard that they deny I exist, sort of like Christmas never happened, though there are still people who celebrate with trees.

I've tried to confine my mind to where I work and ensure that there is a certain grace to retrieving bowling pins in Howell, NJ.

The Austrian no longer works with us and has been hired by the dermatologist to extort mothers who refuse to give their children hormone shots.

"It's not extortion," the Austrian told the local newspaper, "the mothers are merely negligent and we need to prepare everyone for the next hurricane."

I imagine that the girl with the beautiful face, when she wears makeup, is wearing even more makeup than she did in college. Some might consider this surface beauty, but I believe in the ambiguous nature of her refinement.

MRS. ROSEMONT

Mrs. Rosemont was more impressive than her daughter. Mrs. Rosemont was my speech coach in third grade, and if it weren't for her, I would have slurred my words and tripped over speeches and never made it to the forensics team.

When I was fifty years old, I started dating her daughter Emily, though we had never spoken (but always knew one another).

Mrs. Rosemont said she was a lesbian, but was married to a man, which meant you don't have to be with a woman to be a lesbian.

Emily also believed she was sometimes a lesbian but would switch her sexual orientation if it became unpleasant.

When I visited Mrs. Rosemont after my breakup with Emily, I chatted with her son, Marcus, who is sweet, cheery and remarkably kind.

Marcus doesn't care what his old family thinks of his new family or his economic triumphs. That is why he lives far from them.

Marcus and I knew each other in high school and he treated me like family, because his own family, including Emily, made him sleep with their German shepherd when he rattled their nerves.

He didn't want to be the brother of Sylvia Plath (aka Emily), and often hung with me, because I was more like an Easter bunny.

When Marcus became an adult, his family was still mentally unstable, and he continued to distance himself—geographically as well as emotionally.

When we saw one another, Marcus hugged me, though I didn't love his sister, or more clearly, she didn't love me, which is why we broke up.

I heard Emily had a new girlfriend, a Hispanic woman, who wore her hair like a lily pad.

She and Emily met over tea, finding their deeper selves in one another.

Emily told people who knew us that we had *never dated*, had only had "part-time moments," moments that could be recorded in a thirty-minute video.

I conversed with Marcus and Mrs. R, but never looked at Emily.

I also informed Mrs. R I had to sell my bike, to whoever wanted it, even for twenty dollars, because I kept falling off.

Emily looked at us, knowingly, trying to peer through the conversation.

I avoided her, though part of me was devoted to her (but didn't want to see her with the new girlfriend).

Finally, Emily and the family, including Marcus, were in their car, leaving.

I asked Mrs. R if she'd give me twenty dollars for my bike.

"Agatha," she said and opened the window, "here's seventy dollars." Which was enough money to live on for the week, though Emily was now in the Volvo, with her new lover, and I was making ends meet.

EDGAR SINATRA

H IS NAME WAS EDGAR SINATRA. He called himself that because it was rumored that a truck driver in his father's
plant, whom he believed was Frank, was his biological father. Edgar even went to Tony Bennett's manager's office with a gun
to see if he could get access to Frank.

* * *

Edgar wanted to be Frank. He liked David Bowie, it was true,
but Frank was more his ancestral lineage than Bowie. He sang like
him in West Village coffee shops, and asked Oprah to tell him *he
was Frank.*

* * *

Edgar Sinatra, who wore black leather and spoke during twelve-
step recovery meetings, discussed how his sister, "Liza," had lied,
that she didn't give the proper respect to her father, Frank, and her
mother, Judy Garland. For Edgar Sinatra, though the adopted son
of a coffee franchise owner, contended he was the love child of Judy
Garland and Frank Sinatra. He even threatened to kill me because
he thought I had sold his story to Page Six in the *New York Post.*

This wasn't completely true. I once sold a story about *Us
Magazine* having its Christmas party at Club USA, and the

executives were ostensibly surprised that Club USA was an S&M club, and how this didn't ring true with Christmas. I had also written about a woman I despised and incorporated her into a short essay on rejection. Apart from these items/people, I had never really libeled anyone, certainly none as off the medication as Edgar Sinatra.

For when he was *on* his medication, he really was a caricature of Frank—friendly and happy like a lobotomized serial murderer. But off that vial of pills, he was an itinerant assassin who chased me down Seventh Avenue South while I was in a cab. He also tried to kill my friend Betsy and me several times, and it was only because we invoked our higher power—a Hasidic leprechaun sitting on a Tiffany & Co. blue bar stool—that our lives somehow became manageable. In fact, the police didn't do jack shit except assure us that we would not be immolated, but we *might* be maimed. For legally, in the late eighties, they couldn't imprison a murderer until he murdered; there was no range, however, for how much victimization could be done.

* * *

We banned Edgar Sinatra from our twelve-step recovery meetings because he kept making threats at our meeting.

When not medicated, Edgar would jump off buildings and screech at meetings. "That's my former sponsee," he said, pointing at me. "She's a vindictive, lying cunt. Her name is Agatha. She wears green trousers and is a kike dyke who wants to be a journalist." This was, after all, a program of anonymity.

He also sent my friend Betsy black roses whenever she performed at a cabaret bar, where he was eventually banned for lousy singing and stalking her.

I go to AA meetings where I meet people such as Edgar Sinatra who invariably threaten my life. Twelve-step meetings are, for the most part, places where the mentally ill congregate to hear one another. Some of us more normal folks go there to dispense with loneliness; what happens is that we end up accumulating everyone else's problems; we become shopping-bag women collecting other people's emotional disabilities.

As I said, Edgar Sinatra was okay when he took his meds. He had parties with lox, cream cheese and bagels. Born-again Christians and transgender folks alike were welcome in his Chelsea apartment, which his adopted father, the non-Frank Sinatra who owns a coffee franchise (where Edgar once argued with Bella Abzug over the price of a cappuccino), pays for.

Edgar lived in a kitchen with a Formica table that was an example of his life before he went off his medication—clean. He smiled, he joked, he loved his "sponsees," as he called us. I loved him—he was like a big brother with a large heart and you could always visit him in Chelsea.

* * *

On a sublime but rainy day, George—his real name when he was on medication—went with me to Macy's and purchased a small refrigerator with a lock so that my over-anxious Labrador would not break into the fridge. Edgar, when he was George, was extremely generous and concerned that my dog might develop a severe case of diarrhea from eating two pounds of prime rib in one sitting. "The refrigerator lock is a great precaution," he said.

* * *

I had a dream about Edgar Sinatra recently. He came to me unexpectedly, in the brassiere department of Macy's. Though he wished to murder me, twist my neck with a 36D, that I had unknowingly "ruined his life and sold his story to *Page Six*," he instead offered to help me try on a bra. It was what good friends do.

* * *

After Edgar went off a bipolar combination whose side effects made you rotund, I saw him in an AA meeting in the West Village during one of its breaks when everyone is outside drinking coffee and finding new addictions. The bathroom door was open and you could hear a man peeing with the seat up.

"Please close the fucking door!" I said.

"Fuck you, too!" a familiar voice replied.

He came out, shrieking, dressed as Santa in leather and silver appendages.

"You got a problem, bitch?" Edgar Sinatra spoke, his large stomach sticking out of a red vest. It was summer. He had Santa's beard and hat. He resembled a poodle at a punk rock festival.

"You shouldn't pee with the door open," I said.

"You talking to me?" Santa said.

"Yes, and you shouldn't…"

"Look, you witch, you sold my story to *Page Six*. You better apologize or I'm going to throw this chair at you."

"I'm sorry…"

"Get the fuck out of here! And if you tell anyone, I'm going to kill you!" As I was running out, he howled.

* * *

I received a phone call on Yom Kippur when most of us pay for redemption and do not commit sins. Serial murderers cannot distinguish Yom Kippur from other days.

"Mom," I said, "can you hold on a second? I have a call on the other line."

"Hello?"

"Listen, you kike dyke—*I'm going to kill you!*" Click.

* * *

I have never been fearful of strolling in the West Village, except for when the Bronx gangs made their homophobic presence known along Sixth Avenue in the late eighties. The gangs came down in groups comparable to the flash mobs, and like urban termites, they filled the streets with ire and restlessness.

Other than that, I flew through the streets like a drunk, flying squirrel—maybe a Jack Russell, you might say, who has had too many Jack Daniels. This was, of course, during my drunken moments. Many of them, at least the ones I remembered, were far less nefarious than the sober ones.

* * *

After my confrontation with Edgar Sinatra, in the claustrophobic AA meeting that always appeared as if it would collapse on its surrounding tenement apartments, I walked to the Tenth Precinct.

It was next to "Kim's Video," where NYU students and the supposed underground worked and sold CDs and DVDs. I'd spend hours in there, like most of the West Village, pondering Italian movie treasures from the sixties. It eventually became a Marc Jacobs boutique for kids, but when Marc, too, went out of business, it was transformed into a coffee shop where millionaires might call the police if your small talk precluded them from finishing their pound cake.

I went through the Tenth Precinct's double doors—it resembled a public high school that had not yet been purchased by Donald Trump.

"Hi."

"May I help you?"

"There's a guy named Edgar Sinatra who is stalking me."

"We know Edgar Sinatra," they said. Giggling.

"He just threatened my life and he's probably waiting outside."

"Oh really…he's harmless. He came in the other day to pass out flyers that said he was looking for his father."

"He's a dangerous person," I said.

"He brought subs," the officers said.

"He nearly threw a chair at me," I said to the unshaven female cop, who apparently used a razor. She had not, however, used anything that morning.

"*Nearly* is not the same as *throwing*. Look honey, you can't file an order of protection until you're injured."

I suppose they wanted me to file an order of protection after I was dead.

"He also called me a 'kike dyke' on Yom Kippur."

"*Jooooom who?*"

While the woman was playing with her Rolodex, there were men in the background smirking.

"Ahhhh, he's a cool guy, doesn't mean anything," one of the male officers said. Edgar Sinatra ingratiates himself with men, men in uniform, men in underwear, men in all police stations throughout the city. He liked boys in general, and it was obvious that women—whether Bella Abzug or me—were not recipients of his love.

* * *

Edgar, when he was not off meds, was my AA sponsor. Because of him I stopped attending orgies in an inebriated state of mind that often got me from New Jersey to California without much financing.

Yes, I was a drunk, not a fun one. I was also a sexually active person and a member of Plato's Retreat. I never got horrifying diseases, but my sexual participation was like a dog: whenever I saw a human being, I wanted to hump it.

Edgar brought me to convents and explained that other people lived in other ways and I didn't have to go out every night and use my genitals and/or drink Jack Daniels with ice cubes. "If you want," he said, "you may use your brain."

He behaved remarkably different when the voices in his head suppressed the saccharine-sweet Frank Sinatra.

One night when I was with my boyfriend, a guy who didn't realize he was my boyfriend, we ran into Edgar Sinatra, who threatened to execute me for the seventh time.

Oliver, my non-real boyfriend and I, were standing outside a twelve-step meeting along Houston Street when the man in leather suddenly appeared. Edgar seemed to like Oliver, as in *"like,"* to the point where kissing is no longer on the cheek, and wanted to impress him.

"You sold my soul to the devil—*you whore!"* he said. Oliver retracted to a shadow when Edgar came lunging toward me.

"Get the hell out of here!" he said.

"You talking to me?"

"No, I'm addressing the homeless at their annual convention. Get the fuck out of here, bitch!" He followed me down the stairs and I ran into cab, while Oliver hid behind a chair, which he does when people threaten me—not an infrequent event.

I slammed the door of a yellow cab, where a Pakistani man with a deodorizer that smelled like the Jersey Pine Barrens locked the doors. Edgar Sinatra banged on the window, resembling those monkeys at Great Adventure, which try to grab French fries from the people visiting the safari.

The Pakistani cab driver was quite afraid of Edgar. .

"He is very mad at you!" The driver began singing Hindi songs, to ward off evil, he said.

"Step on it!" I said.

* * *

I was exasperated and checked the shower stall when I got home.

My dog is a miniature golden retriever who would likely have licked Jeffrey Dahmer, not knowing his tongue would be pickled.

There was thankfully no sign of Edgar in the bathtub.

He was also, eventually, banned from AA meetings throughout the West Village, though he'd occasionally show up expressing his constitutional rights.

It was rumored that his adopted parents placed him in a mental institution for forlorn children who believe their biological parents were murdered by their adopted parents. They signed, I heard, an affidavit that said, "Edgar Sinatra can no longer function as a worthy member of society," and had his Chelsea apartment taken away from him. At this mental institution, people told me, he was forced to live a docile life—like Vivienne after T. S. Eliot had her institutionalized.

Now and then I see scary shadows and someone singing, "Fly me to the moon," and fear he might be creeping up on me while I'm buying Chinese food.

He also appears in nightmares, and he's quite nice, fixing me lox and cream cheese or Kellogg's Corn Flakes and is not the least bit hostile.

I do hope, like Odysseus, he finds his real father, even if the dude lives in Hoboken.

LIGHTER FLUID

S HE GAVE MY DOG LIGHTER fluid.
   She said my dog didn't drink it because *she put it there*.
   The dog drank it because it was an accident.
   Well, maybe if you hadn't put it there?
   Whether the dog drank it, this has more to do with you and your dog than me.
   She, who took no responsibility for lighter fluid and its implications, was married to a man who loathed my family.
   He disliked us so much that we weren't allowed to look at him.
   If he came in the room, we could glimpse. But if we did more than that, *she* would not speak.
   She was my sister, the woman who gave my dog lighter fluid.
   When *her husband* came into the room, he looked rarefied—red hair, mascara.
   We looked at the corner of the ceiling, not him.
   Such beauty, you know, you don't want to ignore.
   At my mother's funeral, he said, "You have not lost enough weight. You have more to go."
   It's like the lighter fluid—no responsibility, words that burn and stain and strike at us like matches to gasoline.
   Gazoline, that's how they pronounce "gasoline" in New Jersey.
   In New Jersey they don't do things as in other places.
   They don't ban gays as they do in Indiana—no, they yell at them when they graduate from high school.

She didn't know her husband in high school. They met at a pig roast, when the pig's lips were burning.

Since that moment they have loved one another.

They drink together.

They shun my family together.

He let his dog die. He kept saying, *"Die, Henry VIII! Die!"*

They had a New Guinea singing dog who had been abused on the Lower East Side in New York City. They loved that dog—let it run with their cats.

One day the New Guinea singing dog got hit by a pregnant UPS truck driver on Route 9.

They cried, *she* did anyway, though some considered the New Guinea singing dog "gay"— she would have preferred a "regular" dog, but this dog, she loved this dog.

They offered to watch my dog when I got new knees.

I thought the lighter fluid was no accident, just as blueness is its preeminent quality.

It might happen that my dog, too, would get hit by a UPS truck driver who could not control her hormones.

Now I let my dog stay with a painter whose descendants were Portuguese race car drivers.

My dog, the one who drank lighter fluid, is still alive.

IN THE COFFEE SHOP

I HAVE NEVER LIKED TRENDY GIRLS, though I do like trendy coffee shops.

I refer to girls who ignore me while they are talking on their cell phone, particularly if they are walking fierce dogs.

There is such a girl.

She walks down the sidewalk while I am speaking to a disgruntled Southern man about his estranged, drug-addicted wife who is now with a woman.

This chick with her canines—an aging pit bull mix and an irascible greyhound—strolls closer. We are taking up far too much sidewalk room for a discussion about a redneck drug addict who is being seduced into a lesbian lifestyle.

"Hi," I say to the woman. She ignores me.

"Bye," I add.

I hear her release oxygen—that diaphragm exhalation in high school music class in which everyone, except for the talented singers, fake.

I never feel quite at home outside my favorite coffee shop, where this woman and her canines appear, or inside, where bohemians congregate.

I leave her so I can order my coffee. I am slightly older than the other customers; my voice is not modulated to its inside level; my dog's barking interrupts those perusing Dostoyevsky at their tables, which seem like mini-libraries; my clothing hampers the ability of the clientele to look expensively impoverished. It can be stressful for someone like me who is more like an administrative assistant than a hipster caffeine inhaler.

There are no extensive hellos when I enter.

One of the cashiers, a female barista who said I could never do a poetry reading there, always approaches me with great hesitancy.

"Yes?" she normally asks.

"I'd like an Ice Coffee Americano..."

"Do you want an iced coffee or an Americano?"

"An iced Americano."

"They are two different beverages," she says, as if I am questioning the existence of God.

"Americano with ice cubes," I say.

Her paused reticence normally extends to her red-bearded colleague, who exudes the same religiosity while making the drink. He turns his espresso machine nobs with unruffled seriousness.

When I go inside—delayed because the Southern man is aching over his wife's departure—I notice, by looking through the coffee shop window, that the cell phone woman, who ignored me on the sidewalk, has placed her dogs at my favorite bike rack. It is imperative not to raise your blood pressure in public, but it is rather ignoble when other dog owners steal your dog's bicycle rack. It is equally dishonorable for you to not remind the owner that upon exiting the coffee shop, she should not go near your dog, who is now parked further from the coffee shop—his regular spot being usurped—and that he might not be in a position to defend himself if her vicious beasts attack him.

The irresponsible dog owner is conversing on her Samsung Galaxy in the coffee shop, which has received the top prize in the United States for its ability to use grounds in compost in upscale gardening competitions.

"Excuse me," I say, wanting to remind her that she should keep her dogs away from mine.

"Excuse me..." my politeness gets louder.

She continues speaking on her cell but has started waving her hand in my direction, like, "Yo, I'm talking to fucking Jared Leto... *what the hell is wrong with you?*"

I re-engage, "Excuse me, could you make sure that your dogs…" She disses me in front of those drinking coffee and reading Jack Kerouac.

This is the third time she waves her hand in my direction, and since I am no less tolerant of mafia thugs who pet my dog without permission in front of Starbucks, I spurt out, "Fuck you!" The stillness in the café is icy.

"Excuuuuuuse me," the cashier, the one who thwarted my poetry reading, interjects.

"She's ignoring me! Her dogs might—"

"Excuuuuuuuuse me." She is irate. This is worse than calling coffee by its wrong name.

"I'm sorry, it won't happen again," I say.

"It better not…"

There are taciturn customers brooding behind me on line.

"Don't you think this is a double standard? She disdains me but you…"

"What can I get you?"

I order my Americano with ice cubes.

"She's a good customer," the barista says, "and we *treat all our good customers well.*"

I get my drink and while going toward the milk I see the owner, a twenty-ish man. He is always sweet, though I fear he suspects I have a crush on his wife.

"Hey, I'm really sorry—am I banned?"

"Nooooooo—really it's—"

"Are you sure? You guys still love me?"

He nods and tries to be cool. There are payers throughout the room observing him.

"Well, I guess I'll be going," I say.

"Okay," he says. He smiles, hoping that a South Philly Elvis will not be replacing me in the next twenty minutes.

I put my milk in the coffee. I decide whether it is a "Splenda" or a "brown sugar" day.

I see if my dog is still there.

Finally, I exit, looking toward my favorite bike rack, and notice that the girl who has been snubbing me has already left, and that my dog is perfectly fine.

RETREAT

OTHER STORIES INTERRUPT ME, THOUGH I'd like to finish my book.

This one concerns Pam, who bears the same name as the woman I'm obsessed with on a TV show.

We were in Israel in my dream last night. We are either always in Israel or Belgium, where we never leave our hotel or neighborhood, never venture where real tourists go.

We see the circumference of the block.

We read signs and hear that other people are doing fun things.

Some Luddites from high school are residing with us.

Pam, who was the administrator for dead animals in high school biology class experiments, is in charge of health conditions at our retreat.

We are disinterested and consider this the last retreat.

We let our dogs run through areas that would normally be prohibited.

I, for example, let my dog enter the eating area. There are refrigerators that contain shrimp.

In his post-adolescent years, the dog became intrigued with eating shrimp.

Cooked cold shrimp crunches.

Clean, fresh red-and-white meat that could be candy cane if it were not shellfish.

Pogue, my dog, sticks his mouth in the fridge. Pardon me, it is his paw. He extends his paw and hands himself five shrimps.

Pam is overseeing the kitchen, and immediately reports us to a committee, which requests our presence.

I think, sort of, if you have a crush on someone, they're not supposed to report you and/or your dog for eating shrimp.

"It's not sanitary, and I had to tell them that your dog…"

It's how my psychiatrist, whom I also have a crush on, treats me, like she owns me.

"Ms. Ravine," she says, after six sessions, though she could call me "Agatha," but likes the way "Ms. Ravine" sounds on voicemail.

"Ms. Ravine." Pam mocks me, as if I am her servant. "You shouldn't let your dog eat shrimp that doesn't belong to him."

Their words, they think, are divine.

Pam narks. *Would the shrink nark?* If I have a crush on you, you're not supposed to nark.

This philosophy is not always sound.

"I am not thrilled by you, Pam," I say, while Pogue refuses to let Pam pet him.

She stares while we walk away.

Pam saunters after us.

We notice this person by her smell.

Our betrayer is stalking us.

A quiet moment, like rain drops in a Van Gogh drawing, follows, and Pam kisses our cheeks.

We have wanted to kiss since high school, when she was my teacher.

It is an alluring kiss.

It is the only thing that works.

WHIZZING

ABIGAIL THE DOG PREFERRED BUMPY, unapologetic tar and the smell of garbage to this bleak excursion through the blizzard. The roads weren't ploughed and a tumultuous and penetrating wind blew though her ears. She felt the Catskills entering her insides. She'd only been there once, when it was wintry and bitter and freezing.

Abigail's owner, Arthur, a peculiarly inane creature with a red moustache, impatiently dragged her for a walk because he was late to a Debtors Anonymous meeting. This fucking dog would not go on the snow and it burned him up. *Poontang gets eaten up at meetings if you don't get there early—so why won't this runt pee or shit?*

The flakes were coming down heavy and Abigail felt millions of white wet dots on her back and red snout. It was below zero and Arthur had not purchased a coat for her. She was trembling. There were passersby who shook their heads as the skinny beast and the overweight owner meandered.

Arthur yelled at Abigail who refused to go. Not in this skittish weather with this ambitious asshole who wants to go to his fucking DA meeting, she thought. The dog, who was brown and had a blue collar, was shivering. Abigail couldn't defecate and was unclear on how to compensate. She thought maybe, maybe, when this prick leaves this evening, she could do it on his bed. He'd throw her out the window, but at least she would not have to endure his cow-like shouts.

Arthur occasionally hit the dog, particularly if she moved slowly. She reminded him of movie horses that were supposed to budge if you hit them. This time he reached for the leash, although other moments, if it was dark out, he'd get his belt.

Abigail blinked and looked up sheepishly at him. She loved Arthur somewhat but he was being a bastard. If she could, she'd have removed his arms so he couldn't hit her. Abigail recently bit Arthur when he tried to steal a rawhide. Abigail could also not comprehend why, if Arthur doesn't eat the rawhide, he steals it. Abigail had been on the couch, and Arthur despised when her saliva got on his pillow, so he reached for her bone. She then pierced his skin, so this must be why he's angry.

Abigail got uneasy when it snowed. She liked walking on the ice if there was no salt because salt made her paws bleed. This blizzard made her nervous. The dog could not urinate and Arthur was impatiently waiting to see yellow in the snow. Maybe Abigail couldn't think straight with this white mixing with slush where she normally walked over empty soda cans and nibbled on dirty French fries. She also couldn't see Chinese people who normally covered the streets in her neighborhood. Several times she noticed that Arthur, trying to get through the Asians, had ignited near riots. It was a rare moment when she wanted Arthur to return quickly.

Arthur hit Abigail again with the leash while a neighbor looked.

The woman hollered that she was going to call the ASPCA— that she had seen him do that before.

Arthur told the bitch to mind your own fuckin' business. She was probably a liberal asshole. Indeed, Arthur was prepared to have *Abby sick this cunt if she kept yelling*—especially during the frigging snowstorm.

Abigail did not want to wound her potential dog rights activist and bent down. She scrunched her forehead, which looked like a wrinkled stuffed animal. She squatted, a whiz came through, and she relaxed.

GOD AND
THE JACK RUSSELL

THE JACK RUSSELL BIT HER owner. *She's humongous and eats more food than I do. I want chicken breasts, not this lamb/ rice shit. Okay, she mixes it with Parmesan cheese—big deal. Nothing tastes better than poultry parts dipped in succulent* schwartza[7]*-prepared barbecue sauce. That's one thing* schwartzas *are good at—barbecue sauce.* The owner sensed racism, and had read somewhere, perhaps on the internet, that Jack Russells had chased slaves who escaped Alabama plantations during the 1800s.

The owner was upset because cockroaches ate most of the lamb/ rice, which cost her $25.99 a bag—on sale! She contemplated using the methods of an ex-PETA activist who water-boarded her cat for taking a dump in the laundry hamper; water-boarding the roaches might hinder their unwanted consumption.

The dog, with a black and white face and green/hazelnut eyes, stared at the neighborhood's trajectory of travelers who passed underneath the window. She looked dejectedly at the ceiling or played with decapitated toys.

* * *

---

7 "Schwartza" is a derogatory Yiddish term for African Americans.

The Jack Russell had a small Marmaduke toy that she received for her seventh birthday. She loved "Marmy" and with the skinny brown toy pretended they were male canines dressed as "dog queens." Marmy and her lover wore White Diamonds perfume and sniffed each other's butts.

The Jack Russell and her owner normally walked to Walgreens—and then a little further, after the owner joined the Lose Weight Club at work. They eventually traveled beyond the Walgreens garbage dumpster after the owner's doctor advised, "Stroll to prevent a stroke," but they rarely went around the block. This, of course, led to the Jack Russell bouncing/trouncing throughout their small apartment, causing indentations in the wall.

Without good food and long walks the Jack Russell was depressed. This also led to negative revelations about her lover: *Marmy is not very sexy—he's too small and I do all the work. I'd prefer sex with Sweet Polly Purebred!*

The owner saw the dog's diminutive facial expressions and drooping eyes and caressed her teats. The owner surmised: I'll scratch her belly and go to work—where I administer grammar vaccines[8] to incompetent financial writers—and come home to dog kisses. What a life—words and tongues—she thought, as she opened the door to leave.

However, this day was different from others. The owner forgot to turn the radio off and could not predict that the radio announcer would switch from jazz disc jockey to anti-homosexual Pentecostal minister.

The Jack Russell was always distressed by her owner's departure. She lowered her head, drank water from the bowl, and heard a deep and unhesitant voice resonate from the static channel: "The ruin that homosexuality is wreaking upon Native American Indians is devastating; these reservations are no longer conspicuously heterosexual and happy places. If we all pray, Jesus will destroy these infidels by sending them to Hades tomorrow

8 Contains 0.5 mL of *The Chicago Manual of Style*, with 0.2% alcohol-based words from E. B. White.

morning. It is unthinkable for man to fornicate with man and woman to go downtown on woman. Would a Jack Russell have sex with a German shepherd?" he yelled to his disciples—the studio audience jubilantly responded, *"Hell, no!"* This terrified the Jack Russell, who occasionally, when walking near Walgreens, sniffed a German shepherd who barked like a broken pencil sharpener.

The minister's voice blew through the Jack Russell's upturned ears. The little beast was soon consumed with Jesus and hedonistic German shepherds and Native Americans who were victims of homosexual-manufactured crystal meth (cooked in high-end factories on broken floors in Albuquerque, New Mexico, that rested above cockroach-infested pizzerias, the Pentecostal leader declared).

The canine guiltily thought of Marmy. *This minister, who asks his followers to denounce gayness as some might oxygen, would not approve of dog queens.* "The Lord will not tolerate faggots or dykes!" Obviously, the animal felt, this must apply to canines and their synthetic lovers.

The dog, terrified by the speaker's rising decibels, reached for the headless blue/white teddy bear. She pushed the teddy bear and a red-haired Barbie doll together; she manipulated her toys into the shape of a cross. *If Jesus means anything to me, I must do this exercise and receive his blessings, which I do not get from Fatso. She starves me like an imprisoned member of the IRA. Her walks are equal to the length of a four-inch treadmill.* (The Jack Russell detested the short strolls, but obsessively sniffed items in the Walgreens garbage dumpster, which became their destination point. Now and then she ate a chicken bone from the Islamic chicken store across the street that catered to cab drivers who did not permit either her or the owner to drink coffee in their café because she was "neither male nor Muslim," she thought. In addition, the dog sometimes imagined that Arabs were African Americans and barked so loudly they spilled their Moroccan coffee.)

The Jack Russell shoved stuffed animals and one cotton boomerang into her crucifix sculpture—this made her relax; Jesus might forgive her for the sin of having sex with Marmy and lusting for Sweet Polly Purebred. *Marmy doesn't kiss well; when I reach for her tongue, I choke on cotton threads. And Sweet Polly Purebred is obsessed with a faggot named Underdog; her lust is like straight women throwing panties at Liberace in the sixties.*[9]

The Jack Russell made her sacrifice to Jesus. She knew the owner was Jewish, but it was implausible to construct a Star of David—it was stressful enough to do this Toys R Us crucifix, let alone design a sculpture for the chosen people. *No—this ain't happenin'*, she decided, *I have finally found the Lord and am going to achieve sirloin steak salvation in the afterlife.*

As the dog motioned (via snout) a beheaded Snoopy to the top of the crucifix, she heard the door open. It had been hours since the minister first frightened her into salvation (he still shouted from the portable radio). As she completed the crucifix, *Fatso* opened the door.

"What have you done to my living room?" The owner peered quizzically at the little canine, who stood proudly in front of her Pentecostal offering. The owner had never seen a cross this large, let alone one that comprised her dog's entire toy collection.

She stared at the pile, where platypus met rhinoceros. There was a Dodo bird in the middle. Marmaduke, who normally maintained a position next to the canine's throne/bed, was at the bottom of the structure. Unlike Beatrice in Dante's *Divina Commedia* who reached heightened levels in *Paradiso*, Marmaduke was in the bowels of the *Inferno*.

The master listened to the evangelist's voice, "Either you give yourselves to Jesus or to a German shepherd."

*   *   *

---

9 The Jack Russell was not alive during the sixties, but heard that when Liberace visited Durham, North Carolina, in 1962, the Daughters of the American Revolution organized a Fruit of the Loom collection for him.

This must be the correlation, the logic, the owner thought, which has brainwashed my dog into creating this disconcerting sculpture in our studio apartment. She turned off the radio.

The Jack Russell, who normally licked the owner, scarcely moved.

"Don't you want Marmaduke?" The owner disrupted the sculpture's permanence and removed Marmy, whom she placed next to the sneering Jack Russell.

"Are you anti-Marmaduke?" The Jack Russell continued to sneer, as if, on the Pentecostal minister's behalf, she might snap at this Jewish female.

"What you need," the owner quickly motioned to the leather leash hanging on the wall, "is a walk..." The "walk" word caused the Jack Russell to forget her newly acquired religiosity. She jumped toward the owner and aligned herself with the leather leash.

They went toward the Walgreens garbage dumpster. The Jack Russell enjoyed garbage although the owner feared such waste matter might corrode the canine's insides. Nonetheless, to the owner this was preferable to a mile-long stroll or the intersecting toys in the living room.

The small dog feasted on a selection of SPAM and frozen pizza crumbs. Her dexterity was such that she could ingest food before the owner could retrieve the unsavory smorgasbord from the dog's esophagus.

"Do you realize that SPAM is a culinary delight in Hawaii?" she asked the Jack Russell.

The Jack Russell barked, as if she and Jesus were finally at ease, and looked forward to future kissing sessions with Marmaduke.

WHEN HERRING GULLS
WANT TO FEED

WHEN HERRING GULLS WANT TO feed their babies, they regurgitate.

This is how Maurice gets fed.

Agatha eats wonton soup with roast duck.

* * *

Agatha visited her brother Bruce in Michigan. He was disgusted by her behavior.

* * *

Maurice licked SpaghettiOs from Agatha's mouth.

Maurice wasn't like his grandmother's dog who ate feces.

* * *

"I can't believe you did that..." Bruce said.

"Did what?"

"You spit up your miso soup and drank it again...that's *gross*..."

"Well," Agatha said, "our Daddy did it."

"Daddy never did that..."

"He did...."

Agatha washed her sushi down with a Coke and brought it up again. She repeated the process three times. Her food had a spongy taste, like chewing gum but meatier.

"If you don't stop I'm going to leave..."

* * *

Agatha ate Salisbury steaks in high school and vomited them but didn't think people noticed her.

* * *

Regurgitating, which was more low-key in its use of the esophagus, Agatha thought, was an abbreviated version of vomiting. It didn't punctuate and pulverize.

Plus, spitting up food relaxed her.

It was a snack box that you could get from your esophagus.

* * *

Bruce got up from his seat.

"Where are you going?"

"I'm leaving...*you're disgusting...*"

"Are you paying the bill?"

He didn't answer.

* * *

Bruce spat on the floor.

His dog ran to lick it.

"That's disgusting!" he said.

The dog jumped on the sofa, batting the cushions with his tail.

* * *

Maurice vaulted toward her.

He licked the teardrops.

"You love me more than my family and I love you," Agatha said.

She stared at Maurice.

Maurice continued licking her face. It's salt, he knew, but she'll give me food later.

SKULL SESSION

THE JEWISH PSYCHIATRIST LOOKED AT Hitler and a photograph of Henry Ford above the Nazi's head. Hitler had smuggled him in from Auschwitz. "Jew—do you know why you're here?" the Führer yelled from behind his wide mahogany desk.

"I'm at your service," the man said. He was wearing a blue uniform that was on the upscale side of concentration camp. Hitler, dressed in his Nazi uniform, told Himmler, who was responsible for the SS, to bring him a shrink in clean attire, "Not a tie or suit because I don't want him to think he's human." The Führer did not shake the man's hand but nodded.

The psychiatrist tried not to look too intensely at the photograph of Henry Ford, who, like Hitler, was known to be a rabid anti-Semite. Ford's four-volume book, *The International Jew*, had influenced Hitler's *Mein Kampf*.

"He's one of my heroes, though he's American. Do you know why you're here, *Jew?*" Hitler threw his leather whip on the desk. He'd been exceedingly mistrustful since July 20, 1944, when his officers tried to blow him up. The conspirators had been executed, but Hitler had a lingering suspicion that the Wehrmacht would do it again. The army never accepted him into their coterie and referred to him as "the bourgeois corporal." "Did you hear me, Jew?"

"I'm sorry, Mein Führer." The former psychiatrist, who had been starving for months, barely fit in his clothes, which fell off him. "I'm at your service," he said. His whisper was not as high as the bulb hanging above.

The psychiatrist, Hitler noticed, was tempering his words. He was bald and weighed eighty-five pounds—a good weight for someone working with rocks since 1941. This prisoner, originally known as Dr. Schmidt, was renowned for developing personality disorder theories with Freud, who left Germany before the Nazis took power.

"People are trying to murder me!" Hitler yelled. "If you can't help, you'll burn." The psychiatrist, whose name was now Number 100034 (indicated by the bluish tattoo on his arm), trembled more than the twitching dictator in the leather chair. Number 100034 turned pallid on a wooden stool, which would later be sterilized with Lysol.

"What makes you think this?" The skinny inmate looked carefully at the Nazi leader.

It was unfathomable, Hitler pondered, that a man who had been starving since the early forties could remain so articulate. Indeed, Hitler was impressed that Number 100034 retained any sense of professionalism.

"I don't think this—*I know* there are people out to get me!" Hitler said.

The shrink bowed. "I'm s-s-sorry you feel that way..." His words, Hitler discerned, were as fragile as his bones; his skeleton was protruding beneath the skin.

"I trust nobody—you understand that?" Hitler, whose pharmaceutical intake made him irritable, grabbed the whip. Blondie, his dog, strolled in and lay down. She licked Hitler's hand and sniffed the frail psychiatrist.

"*Setz!*" Hitler said as the canine growled, but the master did not silence her.

The shrink was squinting. *Perhaps,* Hitler thought, *this invertebrate once wore glasses, because he doesn't look straight at me.*

"Perhaps it is more *what* you fear than reality," Number 100034 said.

"Did you not hear me, *Jew*—these people nearly blew me up." Hitler scratched his moustache. He knew his enemies were obsessed with him and couldn't understand why this anorexic fellow did not comprehend that the Führer was the solar plexus of humanity.

"Do you not see I am in charge—that these were my generals— that I cannot trust anyone?"

"Maybe," Number 100034 said, "these men are like the children in Linz who used to follow you, but are now taking a different path." The man breathed heavily. Himmler assured Hitler this was a healthy specimen.

"Did you have a good relationship with other kids?" The doctor was trying to deflect some of the Führer's anger.

Hitler deliberated. In Linz, he was popular and the boys followed him when they played cowboys and Indians and read comic books. His mother doted on him. It wasn't until he met Jews in Vienna that he became insecure.

"How was your relationship with your father?"

"He was strict." Hitler moved uncontrollably—he was suffering from Parkinson's, which was likely caused by the cocaine and speed his physician prescribed.

"When male authority figures are domineering," Number 100034 said, "we fear members of our own sex."

Hitler couldn't determine if the prisoner was desperate or helping him.

The Führer had not been not in therapy since he was eight, when his grandmother questioned his soul. She sat with Hitler on the porch and asked if he felt birds running through. He silently nodded, drank his lemonade and ate strawberries with whipped cream.

"How many sessions will I need?" the Führer, petting Blondie, asked. Hitler also thought of Himmler's involvement, and worried that the SS leader would inform other cabinet members.

"That depends on you," Number 100034 answered.

"This may ensure your survival." The Führer meant that Number 100034 would be housed in a more civilized concentration camp than Auschwitz. Hitler, his hand trembling, grabbed Blondie, "Are you still a Freudian?"

"I'm not. I do not believe in *all* his theories." Number 100034 suppressed another cough. Hitler wondered if the man had TB and considered how he would scold Himmler for subjecting him to this. Hitler leaned against the wall in his swivel chair and put his polished boots on the desk.

"Freud was the Jew-dictator of psychiatrists," Hitler announced to this man who was not taller than five and a half feet—smaller than the Jewish corpses in formaldehyde displayed in tanks in eugenics classes at Friedrich-Wilhelms-Universität.

"I'm sorry, Mein Führer, I do not know Freud's current theories." Hitler thought ruefully about his father who used to beat him.

"Do you think I'm unreasonable or that these men really want to murder me?" Hitler said.

"If there was a bomb that almost destroyed you—it's probably not paranoia. But I believe these fears begin in our childhood." The man scratched his forehead, which had recently been crawling with lice.

Hitler asked his guard, who had been in the foreground, to bring the former doctor some biscuits. The shrink hungrily ate them and drank the water provided. He looked up slowly at the Führer, who was sipping a glass of ice water and staring impatiently at him.

"Do you believe that this assassination added a new layer to my paranoia?" Hitler blinked.

"If people are trying to kill you, it adds an entirely new dimension to your stress level," Number 100034 added, removing crumbs with his finger. He folded his hands together and kept his head lowered.

"I hope our next session will be more productive." The Führer did not touch the prisoner-therapist's hand but signaled for the guard to take him away. Blondie followed Hitler into an adjoining room, where they climbed into bed.

GOLDA MEIR ON THE BUS

WE MET ON THE M4, where my friend Q took a photo of us, me and Golda, hugging.

My mother was proud. If her daughter's got to be, *you know*, God forbid, but if she must, it might as well be with Golda.

Mrs. Meir and I had feelings, that is, between us.

I could sense that Golda had my depth and I had hers all these years; and few, perhaps many, knew she had feelings for me, or women, but especially me, because we fell in love in Manhattan at two a.m. when we were riding the M4 on the Upper East Side where you can see the river.

We walked home together near the wired fence.

My mother would love Q's Polaroid, so I brought it to her restaurant.

An ex-girlfriend and old nemeses were there. *Nemeses and exes are always jealous of you and that is why they are what they are.*

The *ex* wore a white hat because she had just graduated from cooking school. She was overly excited by her own existence, and I couldn't muster a word or two, though we sat at the same table.

When Nemesis #1 saw my picture, she replied, "Oh, Golda has posed with several of my friends on Kibbutz Gezer," which is where they grow carrots in places not uprooted by tunnels constructed by Hamas and funded by Iran.

Nemesis #2 was not the least bit impressed with my new inamorata and ripped up the photograph, which was like removing an irreplaceable rib or tearing off a year's worth of work on your resume.

She didn't care, Nemesis #2, and I punched her in the face.

No one at the table, including my ex, bearing her chef's hat, could comprehend why I would punch her.

"She destroyed my Golda," I said.

I tried to repair the damage, you know, use tape or Elmer's Glue, but Nemesis #2 was dead set on preventing this—she jumped on me.

Finally, three Israeli security guards, who were always present whether Golda or her photographs were around, tackled Nemesis #2, who had been hounding me since the time she requested I pick up a used condom in front of everyone in our high school cafeteria.

Nemesis #2 was on the floor.

The Israeli guards gave me my pieces.

I looked to see if they would make a puzzle, which would be good enough to impress my mother, but they were just scraps that I held in my hand, which would now and then help me recall Golda on the M4.

BECKY AND SPINOZA

Becky Kerr never struck me as a member of the North Korean Liberation Army.

Becky organized great celebrations, which were supposed to delete all memories. They did not.

All of Becky's friends, including me, stopped talking with her after she deflated the tires on her ex-boyfriend's car. We felt, "It is not good to take aim at your ex-boyfriend's tires."

Each time I'd visit her hometown, Hobokenoake, I'd refuse to see her.

She sent several people who offered me a ride to her house.

I refused.

* * *

One day, while we were drinking decaf lattes in Café Hobokenoake, Becky walked in with her new friends. They were Chinese, though she claimed to be a member of the North Korean Liberation Army. "These people fund us, and you know how it is with the sponsors."

We were scared, as Becky had given our names to both the Chinese and the North Koreans, and all future attempts to be free would be diminished, should we step beyond the borders of Beijing or Pyongyang.

* * *

That she was demented was always apparent, particularly when she kidnapped me on her green farm and asked me love to her again, though I hadn't felt anything for her since observing her mother eat pimento cheese sandwiches.

* * *

My mom, who was pleased that Becky let me do laundry at her house, wanted me to give her another chance.

* * *

It was too late.

The North Koreans had taken over.

We would never watch ambiguously satirical East European films again.

The question of imperialism would always be a closed argument.

The delineation between Pimento cheese sandwiches and her new love of kimchi would be devoured by her incipient love of Pyongyang.

I would be fearful that a red rocket would kill me from the clouds.

This was much worse than my lack of forgiveness for the flat tires.

But more fearful than North Korea and China was Becky's own unpredictable personality.

* * *

She had stalked into my bedroom while me and my boyfriend were making out.

"Do you think Spinoza believed in Jesus?" she said. This was not an appropriate conversation before or after orgasm; even during, yes, I'd have second thoughts bringing this up.

"So, about Spinoza," she said, with my boyfriend, shocked, standing naked in the corner.

I told Becky to get back into her Pontiac. We'd discuss this later.

* * *

Since her departure for Pyongyang, she has not been seen in Hobokenoake.

We think she oversees a North Korean version of the Brownies as "The Dear Leader" is a fan of American culture.

"I was always a great Brownie," I remember her telling me, whereas I only inherited my cousin's Brownie medals.

And yet, there she is, Becky, somewhere over the clouds, better friends with The Dear Leader than any of us could have imagined.

EZUREEKAE

HELENE AND I MEET ON a site where people are not permitted to be flabbergasted. We are required to maintain low blood pressure, and once our blood pressure levels are approved by Buddhists at Bennington College, who also okay all connections on this site, we are given access to one another. We eventually switch to using cell phones.

Helene, unfortunately, after we're off the site, believes my phone volatility "destroys her mellow composure." My feeble inability to exercise restraint is so unlike the "the Agatha" who had previously seduced her.

Dear Agatha:

After speaking with you, I realized that we were not raised on the same plot of land.

If you had been born in Jamaica, Queens, and/or excommunicated from my Episcopal Church, there might have been a spark.

It is excruciating, this dating, though I hoped to commune like Beatrice and Dante—at least from Beatrice's perspective. In truth, I have no desire to let you chase me through the streets of Paradiso—you're not Dante, I can't be your Beatrice, nor do I wish you to haunt me.

Best of luck to you!

—Helene

Dear Helene:

When was the defining moment that my maudlin personality got to know yours?

One minute I was providing you with divine inspiration, and thereafter I was not even worthy of a pancake at your table.

As you recall, I was talking from a Greyhound bus when the bus driver threatened eviction from his vehicle if I didn't turn off my cell phone. I explained this, but you were digressive and evasive and clearly unaware that I, too, was on the planet.

You stipulated, before we began our conversation, that you were cooking onions—*you couldn't stay on the phone more than ten minutes but nonetheless kept talking.*

"I've never taken Greyhound," you said, "only the Chinatown bus where I caught a virus—but never took it again. *Don't like viruses.*"

"Yes, well, I have seen both phlegm and drug dealers on those vehicles," I said.

"By the way," you said, "how did you come up with your screen name—EZUREEKAE?"

"It's ancestral."

"Ancestral?"

"I'm from a long line of Crimeans named EZUREEKAE who were bottle washers before the communist revolution."

We then heard vibrations over the Greyhound PA system, which could have been a North Korean countrywide speaker announcement.

"Will the loud individual on her cell phone please desist?"

You kept talking. I wanted to crawl under my seat.

During this static dialogue, there was no way two humans could have decided if their destinies were linked. Certainly not the kind of bathrooms they'd use.

Now that you have rejected me, I wish you much luck in your quest to superficially diagnose future love partners.

Yours in inconsequential desire,

—Agatha

THE DUTCH GIRL

THE MUSLIMS ON OUR STREET sang prayers for me. Everyone on Facebook encouraged me to date her: we were both quirky, and though on different continents, we played Scrabble with slang words—me in English and her, also in English.

The only person, of course, who had doubts, was my therapist, Dr. Samson, who was certain she was a fabrication—she was Mohamed of Tunisia rather than Vivian of Amsterdam.

To begin with, Vivian said she lived in Switzerland, though her office was in England, and that she was from Amsterdam. This seemed an odd transposition of places to accumulate for a paycheck.

"And my lover just died of cancer, so I'm looking for a new one."

"I'm sorry about your loss."

"LOL and thanks."

Between "LOL" and "thanks" I surmised this person might not be who she said she was.

I had already endured, a decade earlier, a woman of Aryan-Hispanic origins who wrote me from Africa (she was originally from Illinois), where she was staying with her sick mother. Our relationship had tidy moments of S&M via Skype, but got insidious when she mentioned her mother's terminal illness; this maternal calamity caused irreparable financial damages, and could I please send $2,500?

* * *

Loneliness can make a Bronx dyke swerve to fake lesbians on OkCupid.

"What do you do for a living?" the Dutch girl asked.

"I'm a meteorologist," I said, because, like me, weather is organized by chaos, and within its chaos there is its own organization.

This sounded better than my real occupation—word processing in the pharmaceutical department at a Bronx hospital.

"Wow," she emailed, "that's cool."

"Yeah, most of my friends hate me if there's a blizzard. I'm like—it's God's mood swing—*not mine.*"

"LOL!" she wrote. When you get an "LOL" while dating, it means things are neutrally fine, there is a possibility you will kiss them, and that in your flannel nightgown, lying on flannel sheets, in weather you incorrectly predicted, you are still in the running for the position of "girlfriend."

When the Dutch girl mentioned she was now living in Madison, Wisconsin, selling laboratory equipment, I was confused.

"Do you think she exists?" I asked my psychiatrist.

"I think you should stick with women who resemble your ex but need plastic surgery."

Yes, in addition to the Dutch girl, there was, on OkCupid, another girl interested in me. This one resembled a former lover, but her face was asymmetrical. "Plastic surgery girl" lived in Manhattan; had an oil-burning stove in upstate New York; liked art and Afghan food.

"You need someone on the continent," he said.

"Vivian lives in Wisconsin."

"As I said," he continued, "it wouldn't hurt to date someone within an hour's distance."

The girl with an oil-burning stove was Jewish, which was a factor that my dead mother and psychiatrist loved. I, however, was more into the Dutch chick, who was originally from Switzerland, had witnessed her girlfriend die of lymphoma in the Netherlands, but was now in Wisconsin.

"You are geographically challenging," I wrote the Netherlander.

"Coordinates well with you."

"Why?" I asked.

"I'm worldly and you're *weatherly*. LOL."

I didn't get her humor, but it might have been a translation issue.

Vivian was a single girl with a simple understanding of life who wore a hat to appear androgynous and other times let her curls fall out so she could yell, "*Godverdomme!*" which was "Goddamnit" in Dutch.

Her friends called her "*gek,*" which, in the Netherlands, means "crazy."

She liked older women, though it was not clear why.

I found her sweet, charming and inscrutably kind, and the geographical confusion issue, which I had discussed with my shrink, sunk into the background during our flirtatious moments.

"What are you doing now?" Vivian asked.

"Thinking about you."

"And what are you wearing?" she prodded, as if it were a nuclear secret that the Russians and Americans were already sharing.

"My blanket!" I texted.

She texted back, "That's sexy!" with a smiley face.

After viewing porn, I'd circle my brain and kindle the fires with her photo. The one with the hat. It was euphoric.

* * *

Some people, like my friend Eddie, do "date in three-dimensional reality," and call their choice "old school," even if it means, as it did for me, meeting drunk poontang in Jersey City women's bars. Though sloppy and wobbly, you know what you are taking home. Or at least you think you do.

I'd bring girls home, read them excerpts from Dr. Seuss's *Fox in Socks,* endear them to my inferior social skills, and get laid. Seuss and Heineken made a great night of fun, and though it was not cyberspace, the reality was that it was over in twelve hours. At least with cyberspace you can endure a fictitious affair for a week.

"I'm not able to sleep at night," Vivian via Wisconsin via Amsterdam texted me.

"Oh boy," I replied, feeling the pangs and intimacies of love through the iPhone, "I wish there was something I could do."

"There is…"

"What dear? How may I give you greater comfort in the evening?" I had already checked out the Priceline.com tickets for Madison, Wisconsin, which were slightly cheaper than Amsterdam.

There was a brief pause. She wrote back.

"Financial."

I stopped breathing momentarily. I thought this only happened once every ten years via the Internet. But it had been ten years.

The Muslim prayers were failing me.

All the support I received on Facebook had been for naught.

"I'm sorry," I wrote her back quickly, recalling the Illinois Aryan/Hispanic hottie who had solicited money for her dying mother in Africa, "I cannot help."

I then deleted her profile and text number from all associated sites and devices.

I proceeded to the girl who resembles my ex but needs plastic surgery; who, though also on the Internet, was a subway ride away. The problem was, unlike the Dutch girl, the girl who needed plastic surgery waited a week each time she responded.

"I'm not having an affair with a turtle," I told my psychiatrist.

"No, reptilian love is not what it's cracked up to be," he said. This must be psychiatric humor.

I said nothing.

"Didn't you suspect that someone who kept switching continents might not exist?" he asked.

I nodded.

"Good night." I went for the door.

"Why are you leaving?" he said. "You have ten more minutes."

"Do you think that ten minutes will transform me?"

I grinned and signed my check.

"Here ya go." I gave it to him. "I'll text if anything comes up."

"Are you sure?" he said. "What about that woman Cindy who wrote you?"

"She puts makeup on cadavers."

"And?"

"She prefers the dead."

"Oh," he said from his seat, the place where he deliberated my life, which frequently came from the Internet.

THE TURTLE

I'M THE GIRL PURSUING THE turtle.

Human girls, who eventually become lesbians, are born during the same period as the immaculate conception of reptiles. Given that they—the mother turtles and Sapphic moms—can't copulate, they give birth to lesbians and turtles who have a kinetic energy that makes them attracted to one another.

She, the turtle's mother, was an incoherent feminist who made a lot of money on the kale market by mixing it with Trader Joe's pita bread and selling it at Coney Island. As a result, the turtle had a nicer existence than I did growing up.

My turtle is not green.

She has brown hair and uses words like "occlude."

She moves rapidly in the dictionary, where she is Ricochet Rabbit on speed going through commas and semicolons and italics—she knocks over accent signs. Exclamation points give her notice.

There are few turtles and even fewer girls pursuing turtles.

She is currently a broad, or was abroad, but is now home, and therefore her texting me, that is the green and grey coexisting, well, this should happen, but she is clearly disturbed by the photo I texted of me with my Algerian friend.

In this picture my cheeks are fat, though I have been eating zero pints of ice cream.

I've been walking to my car, not taking Uber.

When I text her in Spanish, she gets an orgasm.

However, when I contact her in English, with my New Jersey diction flying through the verbiage, accompanied by a photo of me and the Algerian (in a hat he brought back from Tunisia), she doesn't write back.

She likes when I speak in Catalan, you know, using the Google translator.

I also dance grammatically incorrect with a few words in Portuguese.

My own words are not as pertinent.

She is particularly uncomfortable if I go into a diatribe about the South Bronx and its current gentrification.

She is a fan of the former Mayor Bloomberg. I am not. The turtle feels passionate about defending our capitalist mayors, though capitalists may molest young girls in Eleventh Avenue apartments. It might be because she owns a condo on Forty-Third and Eleventh— where an elderly guy once asked me to work in his bedroom.

I remember when I was in this man's Eleventh Avenue bedroom. He said it was his office, "and please make yourself feel comfortable."

He told me to remain on his bed.

My mother said, "Get the hell out of there."

"Are you sure? He's not going to tell the IRS he's paying me. This is perfect for unemployment insurance."

"You get the hell out of there now!" my mother said.

I never collected a paycheck from him, though I worked for two days in his bedroom, and the only inappropriate thing he did was yell at me to leave the living room and go into the bedroom.

The turtle would never molest me, and that is likely the problem.

I would like to put my hand on the turtle's knee during ballet in Lincoln Center.

I want to drive a stick shift and put my hand on the turtle's knee, though I can't.

It is always about putting my hand on the turtle's knees.

Yes, some reptilian creatures, despite their having shells, have an amazing knee structure.

* * *

I call several people and attend numerous AA meetings, even contact an expensive psychiatrist at the University of Pennsylvania. They are all turtle consultants.

"I wrote her seven days ago and she hasn't texted me."

"Well, you know, she's had a rough year," they say.

"She's in Spain now," I reply.

"Maybe Internet service in Catalonia is not as good as Internet service in Philadelphia," a friend, who is a librarian at the Carnegie Mellon library, says.

No one quite understands why the turtle, who has a nerdy disposition and takes notes at my poetry reading, and does not stay afterward to tell me how great I was, runs off like a fly avoiding a swatter, won't sit with me when she arrives at the reading but expects others to sit with her, why this indefatigable creature, who resides in a condo that, when sold, could fund a cult in Santa Monica—why this turtle will not, with a whistle in her mouth and a nose in her ring, text me.

* * *

I look for those greys, periodically, particularly when she is in Spain and I haven't heard from her. I even consulted a guy on a truck who sells underpants for five dollars.

"Will she call? And please don't bang into my Volvo," I tell him this because he is parked inches away from my car. Still, even he, the man who can bargain with the Somalis and Chinese and termite exterminators about the price of underpants in South Philly, can't comprehend that text, a grey thing you see, the words from the turtle, this woman who showed up at the museum with badly colored hair, and why she hasn't written from Spain in three days.

* * *

"Inside voice," she said to me, when we met, on our first of one and a half dates at the Guggenheim for a show about depressed expressionism during the Weimar era.

"That's fauvism," she pointed to the painting.

"What's fauvism?"

"You don't know what fauvism is?" She was perturbed.

"I can look it up on Google," I said.

"That won't be necessary," she replied, though she never gave me the definition.

* * *

We walked outside to a bench.

"Maybe this is the bench where Woody Allen proposed to Soon-Yi Previn," I said.

She smiled, as if Woody Allen should not be on my curriculum.

We couldn't stop talking or I couldn't stop asking questions.

"Why did you get a divorce?" I asked.

"*She* was depressed."

"*What?*"

"She slept in her bed and didn't move."

"Oh," I said.

"I'm going home now," she said.

We took a cab to her house. The place on Eleventh Avenue near the building where the elderly man might have molested me if I hadn't left his bedroom.

She kissed me on the lips as she left the cab.

Just like that. Smooch.

* * *

It must be because I am eating organic peanut butter from a jar. That is why she doesn't like to text anymore. I don't look thirty-five. Your chin gets fatter. You look more like fifty-five than thirty-five even though you are fifty-five, and the Uber driver says, "You are between fifty-five and sixty."

This is the reason we will not get married. She won't come to my cousin's wedding in Toronto. She will remain forever the elusive non-textual girl.

If only I drove my bike to work.

Drank asparagus milkshakes in the morning.

Went to the gym more than twice during my gym club membership.

Indeed, we will not hold hands on the beach in Provincetown and I will use my Labradoodle to meet other turtles.

The thing is, she is a Jewish turtle, and since my mother's death, I've only been interested in Hebrew tortoises.

I hope she writes back, but there is that level of quietness where you feel stuck and no person will convince you otherwise—you are a bad person, which is why the turtle is not talking.

So, you give into the soothsayers, the ones who, after all, have faith and say, "Even if you don't have faith, there is an apparent desire within you to develop that faith, not to claw at your iPad screen, the one she noticed was broken, and that was why you only had one and a half dates."

* * *

I decide it's okay that it's over, that she will never text again.

I'm textless.

Then, after not hearing from her, I send a photo of my dog's paws.

"This is where I achieve inner peace," I jot above the photograph, which shows golden retriever paws under my bed.

An hour later she sends a photograph of her white poodle, in his entirety, and you can see his paws—all four of them, plus his snowy face.

"Glorious!" I text her back, and then it is over. It is over like a nickel that falls into a lagoon.

No retrieval possible.

No more turtles on the beach wondering if you realize they are no longer concerned about you and your lack of an emotional aptitude for these things called relationships.

You are just a stay-at-home mom waiting for your dog to kiss you.

You sit on the bed and relax, anticipating your friends will say something hilarious about Donald Trump.

Nothing, not even good coffee from Boston, will help.

And even if you think she is crazy, and you still don't know what "fauvism" means, your heart aches like a beatnik dispossessed of her edge.

You return to online websites in hope of more turtles.

Dominions and dominions of turtles.

But your head bends. Your mind deteriorates. And eventually you sleep near your puppy.

ACKNOWLEDGMENTS

I'd like to acknowledge the extremely intuitive and hard work of my editor, Margo LaPierre of Guernica Editions; Michael Mirolla, my publisher at Guernica, for believing in this manuscript; my family (Michael, Allan, Stephen, Yvonne, Jess, and the Schachters); the Sweets, Mindy Pitonyak, Randi Levinas, Stephen Peacock, Nancy Viola, Jayne Malillo Wilks, Kelly Lynch, Brian Brunius, Howard Hecht, Liz Kaplan, Pedro Silva, Matt Beierschmitt, Michael George, Andrew W. Monath, Jaime Manrique, Bobby Ward, Cort Bledsoe, Trish Conheeney, Clinton Corbett, Kim Spino, Beth Monica, Janet Capron, Jason Teal, Michele Oshima, Jennifer Wasmer, Robb Quattro, Jeanne Larsen, R.H.W. Dillard, Maurice Ferguson, Wayne Johnston, Katha Pollitt, Cathryn Hankla, Lori Joseph, Brian McCarthy, Eugene Grygo, David P. Stearns, Tom Raul, Tom Holland, and countless others who make the Earth bounteous.

PUBLICATION ACKNOWLEDGMENTS

"Literary Mentors," previously published under the title "Eating Apples," *The Stockholm Review of Literature*, July 2015

"Afternoon in the Living Room," *Prime Mincer*, 2011

"Why Daddy Left Us," *Monkeybicycle*, February 4, 2013

"My Mother Never Liked Me," *Pank*, July 2013

"One Summer I Was a Maid at the Hyatt Regency," *Milk Magazine*, Vol. 5, November 2003

"Inhaling Calvin Klein," *Fiction Southeast*, August 28, 2014

"The Boy Who Used the Curling Iron," *Thrice Fiction*, No. 8, August 23, 2013

"Friends of Mrs. William Burroughs," *Storm Cellar Quarterly*, Volume III, No. 2, 2013

"Peas and Carrots," *Gravel Magazine*, 2013

"The Uninvited Bar Mitzvah Guest," *Hobart*, August 19, 2013

"Amy Q and the Gold Necklace," *The Commonline Journal*, 2013

"Converts," *The Coachella Review*, 2011

"Bestiality," previously published under the title "Peanut Butter, the Dog and Edith," *Kneejerk Magazine*, June 2014

"The Value of Oxycodone," *The Breakwater Review*, January 19, 2017

"Middle," (b)OINK, June 2017

"Hot Chocolate in the Cupboard," *tNY.Press – theEEEL*, 2014

"Extension 501," *Fiction* (Department of English, The City College of New York), Vol. 18, No. 2, 2003

"My Dead Grandmother at the Movies," *Chronopolis Magazine*, July 2014

"The Jew Who Became a Nun," *Menacing Hedge*, (nominated for *2015 Best of the Net*), Fall 2015

"This Girl Maria," *Atticus Review*, September 24, 2012

"Kissing a Tree Surgeon," *S/TICK*, Issue: 2.2, Summer 2014

"She Gave Me a Liberal Dose or When W Invaded Iraq," *The Literateur* (UK), November 26, 2016. Also published in *Facets: A Literary Magazine*, Vol. III, No. 4, October 2003

"Bob and Patti," *Right Hand Pointing*, Issue 115, 2017

"Lavina," *Bull: Men's Fiction*, October 26, 2017

"Horse Carriage and Bed Bugs," *Crack the Spine Literary Magazine*, Issue 160, August 11, 2015

"Embryonics," previously published under the title "Grunt," *Denver Quarterly* (University of Denver), Vol. 37, No. 3, Fall 2002

"The Girl Without Makeup," *decomP magazinE*, February 2018

"Mrs. Rosemont," *Wigleaf*, September 26, 2016

"Edgar Sinatra," *Thrice Fiction*, Issue No. 14, August 2015

"Lighter Fluid," *Hobart*, March 11, 2016

"In the Coffee Shop," *Cigale Lit Magazine*, June 2014

"Retreat," *Thin Noon*, June 2015

"Whizzing," *Midway Journal*, 2006

"God and the Jack Russell," *Prime Mincer*, April 2011

"When Herring Gulls Want to Feed," fiction, *Happy* (The Happy Organization, New York, NY), Issue #17, 2002

"Skull Session," ConnotationPress.com, July 2013

"Golda Meir on the Bus," previously published under the title "Golda on the Bus," *Gone Lawn*, Issue 18, May 2015

"Becky and Spinoza," *Barely South Review*, November 2014

"Ezureekae," previously published under the title "Ezureekae on the Phone," *Foliate Oak Literary Magazine*, 2016

"The Dutch Girl," *Santa Ana River Review*, Volume 3, Issue 2, Spring 2018

"The Turtle," *Faultline Journal of Arts and Letters*, Volume 27, Spring 2018

ABOUT THE AUTHOR

Eleanor Levine's writing has appeared in more than 80 publications, including *Fiction, Evergreen Review, The Toronto Quarterly, Faultline Journal of Arts and Letters, The Denver Quarterly, Spoon River Poetry Review, The Wall Street Journal, The Washington Blade, Artemis Journal, South Dakota Review, Heavy Feather Review, The Breakwater Review, The Citron Review*, and many others. She received an MFA in Creative Writing from Hollins University in Roanoke, Virginia, in 2007. Her poetry collection, *Waitress at the Red Moon Pizzeria*, was published by Unsolicited Press (Portland, Oregon) in 2016. She lives with her brother Michael; their dogs Morgan and Leonard Woolf; and their cats Asia, Snickers, and Raleigh in Monmouth County, New Jersey. She's a full-time medical copy editor when she's not writing.

MIX
Paper from
responsible sources
FSC® C100212

Printed in June 2020
by Gauvin Press,
Gatineau, Québec